I

She was travelling north to see her mother. She had to tell her that she was expecting a baby, and had no intention of marrying the father.

It was still late summer in the big city and the trees there were dark green. Past Sala the sycamores were streaked with red, and by the time she had reached Bollnäs, the north wind had risen and was whipping yellow birch leaves against the windscreen. She turned up the heating in the car.

Her mother was a sensible woman. When she heard that the little shoot wasn't twelve weeks old yet, she would surely start to talk about an abortion. Katarina was determined to refuse. She wouldn't try to explain. Once before she had had a tiny growth scraped away. It was three years ago, and ever since she had been tormented by the thought of not knowing who the unborn child might have been. She hadn't told her mother of the termination then. No point in worrying her – and no point in giving her too much insight into her life.

Had the people in the villages up here in the valley of the river Ljusnan known how she lived, they would think her no better than a whore. There was no denying that she enjoyed being with men and was absurdly delighted at the start of each new affair. Unlike most people, she never confused having an affair with being in love.

'Learning new things to do in bed is so exciting. It's my idea of having a good time,' she had said, laughingly, to someone she had known at school. Her acquaintance had been talking about her marriage and seemed to thrive on her role as wife and mother. Instead of laughing too, she had replied, 'I feel rather sorry for you, you know.'

Katarina had not let her know that this was mutual. She had a mental image of the husband babysitting in the couple's terraced house, waiting and watching TV while keeping an eye on the clock.

They had left the wine-bar and each had gone her own way. But she could not forget what the woman had said. The words were still festering.

Her relationships usually lasted no longer than six months, the average length of her infatuations. That was how she was, and there seemed no reason to change. Yet when a separation was painful, she sometimes wondered if she had run away because she had sensed in herself too much tenderness for the man.

I'm afraid of becoming too close to someone, she said to herself.

And now I want a baby. I want to give birth to a child, suckle it, carry it with me day and night for ever. The thought was so alarming that she had to stop the car. She needed to get out, breathe deeply and persuade her heart to slow down.

She stood in the car park, looking out over the river valley without truly seeing it. As usual, she could feel her confidence seeping away: I will fail, I won't have the strength, won't understand the needs of a child. I'll be desperate to get back to my drawing-board at the office. I'll be . . . The list seemed unending and the conclusion inevitable: I'm going to damage that child where it matters most: I'll sap its will to live.

The wind was tearing at her clothes, and she was frozen. She walked back to the car and sat inside it. Only a few miles to go now. If she spun out this break a little longer, she could prepare better for the conversation with her mother.

Her mother would say, 'You must have an abortion.' She would reply, 'But I want to have this baby.' Then her mother would hesitate but in the end she would say, 'You're not suited to motherhood.' She would screw up her face in the way she always did when she felt cornered into being firm – 'tough for your sake'. She would have plenty of arguments to support her

Elisabeth's Daughter

Marianne Fredriksson

TRANSLATED BY

ANNA PATERSON

First published in Great Britain in 2002 by Orion,
an imprint of the Orion Publishing Group Ltd.

Published by agreement with Bengt Nordin Agency, Varmdo, Sweden.

A CIP catalogue record for this book is available
from the British Library.

ISBN 0 75285 161 6 (hardback) 0 75285 162 4 (trade paperback)

Typeset at The Spartan Press Ltd,
Lymington, Hants
Printed in Great Britain by
Clays Ltd, St Ives plc

The Orion Publishing Group Ltd
Orion House
5 Upper Saint Martin's Lane
London, WC2H 9EA

opinion. Katarina had been scrambling up trees when other girls had been playing with their dolls, had always felt an outsider in the giggling gangs of schoolmates, always thought that babies were repulsive. Every month the wretched business of her period infuriated her.

Eventually Katarina would cave in and return to the big city to have the shoot removed.

The indicator showed that she was turning, but tears filled her eyes and she had a problem seeing in the rear-view mirror. By the time she turned off on to the track that led to her mother's summer cottage, her eyes were dry, a smile was in place on her lips and she felt in control.

She drove up the sloping drive and stopped on the grassed area in front of the cottage. Everything seemed smaller than she remembered it. The forest was slowly but relentlessly closing in on the cottage, the sloe bushes spiky and impenetrable.

Oh, my God, this is so desolate. So silent. The songbirds had fled to the south and those that had stayed had no need of people and bird tables. Even the magpies were quiet.

How lonely it was.

Her mother was outside before she had even engaged the handbrake. The two of them stood looking at each other. It was a moment of pure happiness. Then came the embrace, a long, tight hug that warmed them both.

When they finally let each other go, her mother said, 'Dear heart, you're looking so pale.' And Katarina said, as she had to, that she was tired after the long drive. Tired and hungry.

So her mother replied, as mothers will, 'I have a lovely potato *gratin* in the oven, made with lots of cream. It's to go with brown trout, straight from the stream.' Katarina had no appetite but answered as she had to, smiling as she must, 'That sounds wonderful.'

Actually, all she wanted to do was weep alone.

'You're frozen – come on, let's go inside,' her mother said.

All according to the script, Katarina said to herself. We will never be close. The reason why was clear enough: it was too easy for them to hurt each other.

'Why don't you take your bag upstairs while I get the food on the table?' Elisabeth said.

'Of course,' Katarina replied, but she remained on the porch. The pale blue of the great river had changed to a deeper shade and then to violet along its green and gold banks. The little red houses in the valley were glowing like jewels against the blue of the mountains on the far side. As a child, she had known that the mountains spoke to each other across the valley, telling each other secrets and recalling old fairy-tales. She had wondered how they could speak and asked her mother, who had told her that they had been around for thousands and thousands of years, and that people could not enter their world.

She refocused her gaze and took in the brightness of the afternoon sun on the small panes in the porch window. The scent of lemon came from the pots on the sill. But Dr Westerlund's plants, which were supposed to exude a smell that was good for the lungs, looked dried out and dead.

Katarina went in and stopped again on the threshold of the big room. The faded rugs on the floor were dirty. The sagging armchairs in front of the fireplace were shabby and none too clean, without the red rugs that Elisabeth usually threw over them. The pewter candlesticks stood on the table, as always, but they were empty. The striped runner was not properly ironed and the fat-bellied earthenware pot did not hold the usual bunch of meadow flowers.

It looked odd and sad.

'Supper is ready!' The voice was full of conviction that food was a God-given pleasure.

I can't cope with this, Katarina thought. But later, in front of the kitchen stove with its cosy wood fire, she enjoyed the food and realized with surprise that she was hungry.

I'm eating for two, she thought. Then she told herself how silly that was. The shoot was small and undemanding.

A little later still she heard her own voice say: 'Mama, you must be so lonely up here in the forest. A whole long summer on your own.'

Her mother's face grew serious, and the lines in her face deepened to become folds. She seemed to be looking into herself. 'The loneliness isn't a problem, but somehow I'm not enjoying life as much as usual.'

This frightened Katarina and her heart lurched. 'Mama, are you ill?' she asked.

'No. Listen, I'll try to explain.' She was speaking slowly, as if to emphasize what she had to say. 'I was looking forward so much to this summer. To standing in front of the cottage, watching the cranes flying northwards. To pulling on my boots and walking up along the ravine with the stream. Just listening to sounds, like the call of the cuckoo. Seeing the salmon jump in the waterfall.'

She fell silent, as if searching for words. 'I had been looking forward to enjoying all the spring flowers, the blue anemones first, then the white ones, then the primroses, and – well, you know them all. And then the meadow flowers at midsummer. And, of course, I saw them all, watched everything. And yet . . .'

Her eyes fastened on Katarina's before she continued, 'Maybe the hardest thing to accept was the way I felt when the swallows returned to their nests under the roof. Remember how pleased we always used to be? We'd stand on the steps and sing our welcome-back song for them.'

Katarina nodded and tried to smile. 'But now?' she said.

'Nothing. I just noticed that the usual chattering was going on under the roof-tiles. Then I went into the kitchen and sat down, thinking I'd died somehow.'

The twilight was deepening outside. Katarina said, 'You must have been working too hard, Mama.'

'That's what I told myself, in the beginning. But that's not it. I'm just getting old. You can't stop age taking over. Gradually one's senses – eyes and nose and ears – lose touch with one's heart or soul.'

Katarina's eyes wandered into the blue darkness outside to the edge of the forest, which looked as black as night. Then she collected herself, looked at her mother and said cautiously, 'But I have felt just like you. That I lack vitality and the ability to enjoy things. It's as if life has been reduced to endless repetition. As if everything is always the same.'

'But, Katarina, you're so young!'

'I lead a hectic life, Mama. Sometimes it seems as if there's nothing much left for me to experience.'

The next moment she put her hand on her stomach, as if to establish the presence of her little shoot. Could that be why . . . ?

Later they both felt drained by the conversation.

Elisabeth went for a walk. Katarina washed in a bowl beside the kitchen sink, then grabbed her bag and walked upstairs to the attic bedroom.

They met again outside, standing barefoot in the long grass to brush their teeth.

'Goodnight, Mama.'

'Goodnight, Katarina.'

2

Elisabeth could not sleep. It did not help that her back ached and it was hard to find a comfortable position.

She had known from the moment Katarina had phoned to tell her she was coming to visit that the girl had something to tell her, something that was difficult to talk about.

Not that she had said anything yet.

Most likely she was going to marry that American, and move far away, to the USA. He had seemed an interesting man, with a sharp mind and a good sense of humour. Perhaps a little too charming, Elisabeth had thought when she met him. But that was after she had sensed electricity in the air between him and Katarina.

She had thought it might be serious this time.

Katarina would be full of enthusiasm and talk about how easy air travel was to the USA – planes every day. 'You must come and stay with us in the winter. Imagine being in California, Mama. Back here you'd be in long johns.'

Elisabeth would try to laugh. And she would manage it, of course. She must . . . but . . .

She had seen few really happy marriages, or perhaps she had just failed to notice them. Her own marriage had been sheer hell. The abyss of depression that opened when love died, the insistent insults, the alcohol. The physical abuse, when things got really bad. In the midst of all this, two children had been damaged.

It had ended the usual way, with the Other Woman. She had been younger, born to be a wife and mother. They had had two children together, two boys. If the gossip was to be trusted, he was happy now.

Then she remembered: he was dead. It had been sudden, a heart-attack.

The ache centred on a spot between her shoulder-blades and

the only way she could rest was by turning on to her back. She would never fall asleep like this. There she lay, wide awake.

The problems had started to pile up after she refused to give up her job. Of course she had been in love, but her years at teacher-training college, striving to pass exams, doing the practice sessions and then her first job in a school – all that had been important too. She had to be true to herself.

Against her had been ranged her own mother, her relatives and her husband's dream of a good wife who had supper on the table when he came home.

When the children arrived, she was branded an unnatural mother. That was what her mother and her brothers said. The rest of the family agreed and so did society. Her husband – he who was man enough to support his wife and children – took it badly.

So it was no surprise that what happened, happened.

She turned on to her side and thought about Katarina. She was an architect. They would need her in California. She found this comforting and at last fell asleep.

Katarina was asleep as soon as her head hit the pillow. But she awoke early and her thoughts turned straight to Jack and his wry grin, somewhere between amusement and irony.

This summer had been like no other. The borrowed cottage on a tiny island, the sunshine warming the rocks. The wind filling the sails of their boat. The sea stretching into eternity.

God, how she longed for him.

Then came a painful thought: I cheated him. But not consciously, she countered quickly.

She had forgotten the pills when she went into town. She had planned to phone her doctor, and ask for the prescription to be sent on to the pharmacy in Norrtälje.

But she had forgotten that too. If she had an abortion, he would never know.

★

At daybreak the next morning Elisabeth and Katarina met in the laundry room at the back of the house. They laughed at each other, as they stood stark naked in basins full of water. It was cold, and Katarina was shivering when she wrapped herself in her towel. Elisabeth rubbed her back and upper arms to warm her. The only full-size mirror in the house was there. It was darkened and in bad shape after years of damp and cold. Suddenly they were both looking at themselves in it and giggling.

'It's incredible how alike we are,' Katarina said.

'Don't say that – you're much better-looking than me,' Elisabeth said. 'You always were.'

'Oh, come off it, Mama. Look at us, the long noses, the strong jaw-lines, the blue eyes and the big mouths. Exactly the same features. The hair, too, thick blonde manes.'

'I'm colouring mine.'

'I do too.'

They laughed again. Elisabeth decided that happiness had touched them briefly. 'Let's have some coffee.'

They ran back against the keen wind. The air was glassy, smooth and cold.

Elisabeth had already lit the stove. The kitchen was warm and soon the coffee was brewing, its aroma floating across the table, already set with bread, butter and marmalade.

'You're looking cross,' Katarina said.

'You've always mistaken my being decisive for being cross.'

'So, you've made a decision?'

'Yes. I know you've got something to say and I want to hear it.'

'OK.' Then she said, as she had rehearsed, 'Mama, I'm going to have a baby, but I don't want to get married.'

The logs were throwing out sparks. There were no other sounds in the kitchen and Katarina felt like screaming, 'Speak, for God's sake, say something.' Then she saw that her mother had started to cry: shiny tears were running down the creases in her cheeks, like meltwater streams in spring. 'Are you crying?'

Elisabeth had to swallow a couple of times before she could say, 'Yes, dear heart, tears of joy.'

They spoke no more that morning.

Together they walked in comfortable silence along the path leading into the forest. When they came home, their baskets were full of parasol mushrooms. They fried them, like slices of steak, and agreed that no other mushrooms were so good. They cooked some meatballs too, but the mushrooms would have been enough on their own.

Then they went to their rooms for a nap. Katarina slept like a child. Deeply, beyond doubt and fear. Decisions had been made.

The twilight was deepening and with it came a high wind. The storm blew straight from the north, and the kitchen windows rattled so much that they went into the sitting room and lit the fire in the big tiled stove.

'I had come to an agreement with this man, just as I had with all the others. I told him I had no wish to get married, that all I wanted was to enjoy the time we had together but as a free agent.'

When she had told him this, she had watched his face, and seen first his surprise, then his relieved smile. That charmingly wry smile. It had spread until eventually he laughed. 'You're such a great person,' he had said. Then, soon afterwards, 'I want you to know that I'm married back in the States and have two children.'

It had hurt but she found words to conceal the pain: 'That's fine by me. We can enjoy the summer together and no one will be hurt.'

That's what it should have been like, she told herself. Then she said to her mother, 'You see, the trouble was that I'd forgotten my pills and I only realized as the ship was leaving Vaxholm harbour.'

'*Forgotten* them?' her mother said.

Katarina picked up the emphasis. She considered it for a while and had to admit that her mother was right. 'Well, I tricked him. In a way,' she said.

'And does he know of . . . his good fortune?'

'No, he doesn't.'

The silence lasted quite a while. Elisabeth put some more logs into the stove.

'Normally it wouldn't have been a problem, honestly, Mama. I would have got rid of it. But this time something inside me is telling me I must have this child. It's too strong to ignore or fight off.'

'What if he got a divorce?'

'I would still say no. I don't want to get married. Especially not to a man prepared to sacrifice his career and the happiness of two small children for me. No, Mama.'

'Do you like him?'

'Yes. And that makes it harder.'

They heard an owl hoot in the silence. Both were startled, then they smiled at each other.

'There's still life out there,' Katarina said.

'Oh, yes, and if you're up early enough you can see the elks wandering across the meadow in front of the house.'

'Mama, I thought you'd tell me to have an abortion.'

Elisabeth's eyes were cold suddenly and she flushed. After a moment she said, 'I've had an abortion, you know. It's the most shameful thing I've ever done. I've never forgiven myself.'

Katarina was silent, mostly because she was so surprised.

Elisabeth went on, 'It was after my divorce, when you and I were living in that borrowed flat in Gävle. I had a couple of affairs then.' She saw Katarina's astonishment and laughed. 'You had no idea, of course, but I enjoyed myself, because I discovered what sex could be like. It was a lovely time, full of delicious secrets.'

Oddly enough, Katarina felt hard done by. Ashamed too, somehow. Then she told herself that she was being stupid. 'What was so terrible about that abortion?' she asked.

'Everything. The staff were contemptuous, the doctor was rough . . . the scalpels, the speculum, the piercing light directed into me. Sometimes I think the soul exists in there. For women.'

She had to pause for a while before she could go on. 'The pain. The pain was terrible. No anaesthesia. So much blood . . .' The memories made Elisabeth's face crumple and she looked old. Yet she forced herself to go on. 'Then, for years and years, I was plagued by the question of who she might have been, my little girl who might have been like you.'

'How do you know it was a girl?'

'The doctor told me. I had waited too long, you know. I suppose that's why it all got so . . . bloody.'

Suddenly Elisabeth stood up, shook herself like a wet dog, then said, 'Come on, let's have a brandy.'

The moment passed. Her mother would never know of Katarina's abortion.

They raised their glasses to each other and drank. Elisabeth drained hers. Katarina remembered her shoot and sipped.

'Where on earth did you get the idea that I'd tell you to end the pregnancy? You're an independent woman with a good job, and you live in a society in which single mothers are respected and not unusual.'

Katarina searched for the right words. 'Mama, that wasn't it. It was all about me – the girl who didn't like babies. I still have no maternal feelings. I'm afraid of getting too close to people. I'm just good in bed.'

A lump rose in her throat. She had to force herself to continue. 'I could so easily damage the child, you know.'

'That's what all mothers feel, especially the first time.'

'So you have to learn to be a mother – is that what you mean?'

'The child will teach you. And many of the sensations of motherhood are similar to sex.'

'How so?'

'Babies are sensual creatures, Katarina. They want skin against skin, to be close all the time. You know from your own experience that bodies don't tell lies.'

Katarina's eyes locked with her mother's.

In the middle of the heavy silence Elisabeth started laughing. 'I forgot to mention that the little person in your tummy is going to be much more demanding than any mere man.'

Now Katarina smiled. 'You never were much good at comforting me.'

'Words of comfort are like whipped cream, a superficial topping.'

'That's what you always used to say.'

'Did you miss out on comfort when you were small?'

'Maybe a bit. It just took time for me to learn that honesty was best, even when it was hard to take.'

Elisabeth shook her head. 'Honesty is difficult, Katarina. We hardly know how to handle it at the best of times. People who try to comfort others are usually wanting to protect themselves from their own fears.' She sat in silence for a while, as if she was searching for the right words: 'What I mean by "comfort" is saying or doing something that shows respect for the other's pain.'

'How wise you are, Mama,' Katarina said. 'But all this talk has made me hungry – I need food, comfort food.'

Elisabeth laughed. 'Come on, then, let's go and make some sandwiches. Crispbread and cheese.'

As they moved about the kitchen, the north wind rattled the windows. Suddenly, they seemed to have nothing left to say.

'We'll deal with all the practical stuff tomorrow morning,' Elisabeth said. 'You know you can count on me.'

'I know. Listen, I have a plan.'

'And I've only got one more term to go at college. Perfect timing, don't you think, that I'm just about to retire?'

3

Katarina felt composed, strong and confident, but she could not sleep or perhaps did not want to.

Now, about confronting Jack . . .

She must think it through again, concentrate on the talk they must have. It would not be easy to face him with what she had to say. But she could not focus her mind on it. Instead, memories flooded back. The weekend when Jack first met her mother was replayed in sequences as precise and sharp as if she was watching a film of those days in Gävle.

By then she was living with Jack. They were sharing her beautiful flat in the fashionable Söder district. Jack had said he was curious about her mother. 'You talk about her a lot, you know. What's so special about her?'

'Let's go and see her. Then you can find out for yourself. I'll phone her and ask her if we can spend a weekend with her soon.'

She had chatted with her mother for quite a while, laughing at their private jokes. All this was incomprehensible to Jack, of course. Katarina happened to glance at him at one point and saw that he was quite upset. She started to speak English and told her mother about an American friend she would like to bring with her. 'It will give you a chance to practise your English, Mama.' More laughter.

'What was the joke this time?'

'Oh, just that she's an English teacher and speaks it perfectly.'

The next morning, they found that spring had come while they were asleep. The air seemed to dance, the sun shone and the trees in the courtyard bore flowers on their bare branches.

'Get up! It's a great morning to be alive!' she called to Jack.

'Where's that smell of honey coming from?' he asked sleepily.

'The sycamore leaves are out.'

An hour later they were driving out of town.

'Look! White wood anemones everywhere,' she said, after a while. They're covering the ground in this wood. Let's stop and pick some for Mama. Not even the blue ones will be in flower yet up north where she lives.'

Jack looked baffled but stopped the car and helped her without complaint. It did not take them long to collect a big bouquet. To keep the flowers fresh, Katarina rolled them in pages from the newspaper and soaked it in a stream. 'Look how lovely they are,' she said.

'Ummm. Exotic blooms . . .' Later he asked, 'Do you look alike, you and your mother?'

'We do. Same thick, blonde hair, same high foreheads and determined chins. Same height, too.' She paused, then said, 'Our eyes are different, though. Hers are so light they're almost transparent. Like blue watercolour, diluted to the palest of pale shades. When I was little, I believed she could see straight through people, read their thoughts and even feel their feelings.'

'That sounds rather scary.'

'It was. Then I realized that when her eyes went glassy, distant, she was looking inwards, not at others.'

'Inwards?'

'Into herself.'

'Do you think she'll like me?'

'She doesn't allow herself likes and dislikes. She accepts people as they are, regardless.'

'I'm not too happy about that either.'

'Please, Jack, relax. Anyway, describing your mother isn't easy. Listen, I'll tell you a story – it'll give you an idea of what she's like. It begins at the time when I first fell in love. The best-looking guy in the class asked me out to the cinema. I was madly flattered and really wanted to be in love. I was crazy about him, of course. Back then, seeing a film together meant cuddling and French-kissing in the dark. Never mind the cowboys on the screen or whatever. Hot pursuit, Wild West-style, on the screen and hot fumbling in the back row.'

Jack laughed. He recognized it.

'We were so excited by each other that he came home with me so that we could carry on snogging on the sitting-room sofa. Mama was out. At a lecture, I think. And then there she was, standing in the sitting-room doorway. I'd lost all idea of time. When she had grasped what was going on, she wandered off into the kitchen, closed the door and made herself a cup of tea.' Katarina giggled. 'My boyfriend just about had a fit. Then he pulled himself together, grabbed his clothes and ran for the front door. I went to Mama in the kitchen, but my legs were shaking. You should have seen her – she was smiling at me. She said it was the most natural thing in the world, especially at my age when the body was all tuned up and eager to try everything. She said that when I felt ready for a full sexual relationship, I must tell her and she'd kit me out with contraception, most likely a supply of the Pills.'

Katarina was pleased with her story, but Jack was shocked and he flushed. Neither of them spoke for the rest of the journey.

As they came into the flat Elisabeth shook hands with Jack. 'I'm so pleased to meet you,' she said. 'Why, you look like a real cowboy!'

As an opening line, it was not a success. Jack's smile was even more wry than usual.

She had prepared supper – or, rather, there were ready-made pizzas in the oven, a green salad and a few beers. The plates were set out on the bare kitchen table.

Katarina saw how Jack felt – it was written all over his face: her mother had gone to no trouble at all.

They spoke about how spring was in the air. Katarina produced the anemones and there was a certain radiance about the two women as they stood at the kitchen counter and put the flowers into a vase, one by one, as if they were performing a ritual.

When they were all sitting at the table, Elisabeth said, 'You didn't care for me telling you that you looked like a cowboy, did you?'

'No, I didn't. It's such a stereotype of the American male.'

'Not at all – not to me at least. Not a stereotype, but perhaps an archetype. A cowboy is a hero. He's strong, good-looking, brave and pure of heart. Like the boy who slew the dragon in the fairy-tale, a cowboy is innocent and honest. Somehow, he lives in a world where truth is simple, unambiguous.'

Katarina heard Jack whistle with delight.

She's saved the day, she said to herself, after she had pushed them off to the sitting room. She started to wash up while the coffee was brewing.

Off and on she listened to them talking about Jack's theories on the old cult of the Mother. She had heard him lecture on findings from excavations near Tel Aviv, where figurines of women, the oldest ever discovered, had been found under strata formed just after the Great Flood. 'They had slim, elegant bodies and were painted in red and black,' he explained. He went on to describe the great goddess of the past, and historians' interpretations of her power over souls, which differed greatly.

When Katarina joined them, bringing coffee and a bowl of sweets, he was saying, 'You're responding to this as a feminist. Modern women often do, but it's too simplistic. The key concept was fertility. The miracle of birth was central to their rituals.'

Elisabeth nodded. She hesitated, trying to recall a quotation. Then it came to her: ' "For all men there is but one gateway to life . . . In my mother's womb I became flesh . . . formed from her blood and the seed of man." I think that's from Proverbs.'

'I must write it down,' Jack said.

When he returned with his notebook, Elisabeth said, 'How strange that the Great Mother is making a comeback. Her renaissance is part of a new myth, a scientific one, this time. Which is how we like things. Now the story's about the Good Mother and how enormously important she is to her children. As you know, it is used to tie women to their homes.'

Conflicting emotions played over Jack's face.

They drank their coffee.

Suddenly Jack said, 'I suppose you must know a lot about God and His ways, being a clergyman's daughter?'

'You suppose wrongly. I know a lot about the Bible, but nothing about God. The only God I ever felt something for is Jehovah of the Old Testament.'

'The Lord of the Jews?'

'Himself. He doles out punishments, feels hatred and jealousy, He is power-mad, condemns and destroys. He is the God of Job, as evil as any human being, just less conscious of it.'

Jack almost dropped his coffee. For once he was lost for words.

He wiped the tabletop with a napkin and considered. Then he said, 'If you're right, people in antiquity were better off. At least they had plenty of gods to choose between.'

Elisabeth laughed, and said that neither of them would ever know. Still, maybe polytheism provided better opportunities to create different gods for different ideas. Projecting everything on to a single god made him so contradictory, she suggested.

By the time Katarina and Jack left Gävle, Jack and Elisabeth had become good friends. The following morning, Jack said over breakfast, 'The Good Mother myth is popular in the States. Nothing can compete with it, at least not among the middle classes, and more and more people are buying into middle-class values, these days. The result, of course, is that almost all mothers feel inadequate.'

Elisabeth nodded. Sweden was the same.

'You didn't buy it. You must have been pretty liberated?'

'Not really. There was so much I didn't do, and so much I shouldn't have done.'

A shadow flitted across her face and he regretted asking her.

'I keep telling myself that guilt is part of life,' she went on. 'We must try to deal with it as best we can. The good thing is that morality is its flipside.'

Katarina heard Jack's sharp intake of breath.

Then Elisabeth smiled. 'The other day I read about some intriguing research findings,' she said. 'The study was American, as they usually are. The conclusion was that grown-up children of conscientious "good" mothers are more guilt-ridden than other groups. The children who manage adult guilt best have had averagely good mothers. "Good enough", as Winnicott called them. I was comforted by that.'

She laughed, but Jack, who had never heard of Winnicott, looked grave as they said goodbye to each other.

4

In the morning, the wind blowing around the forest cottage was still chilly. Elisabeth and Katarina had both slept late, though at dawn Katarina had been awake and watched the elks walking across the yard, slow and remote, like creatures from an ancient past.

She heard her mother lighting the fire in the kitchen stove, picked up a pile of photographs and an architect's drawing then went downstairs. 'Mama, look, this is a terraced house in a nice area to the north of Stockholm. Somebody at my office owns it, but he's been after my Söder flat for ages. Now we're talking about a swap.'

'It's quite large,' Elisabeth said. 'Can you afford it?'

'You've no idea what a Söder flat is worth these days. Certainly more than this house. The deal means I'll have money to spare for doing it up – decorating, some furniture, that kind of thing.'

'Good God.'

'And, listen to this, there's a self-contained flat on the first floor. A bedroom, sitting room, kitchen, and a small bathroom. You could have the flat!'

'Good God,' Elisabeth said again.

'Leave God alone,' Katarina said. 'Talk to me instead.'

But Elisabeth made the coffee, and put some bread and butter on the table. 'Now, if there was a garden—' she began.

'Mama, please! Stick to the point.'

'It's usually thought unwise for parents and their grown-up children to live together.'

'Since when did you start bothering about what's "usually thought"?'

'Katarina, this wouldn't be . . . without problems.'

'True. We're too close.'

'I wouldn't know about that.'

'What do you mean?'

'If you trust someone else – for better or for worse – you don't pussyfoot around them, as you do,' Elisabeth said.

Katarina felt anger rising inside her. She drew herself up to her full height.

'Look who's talking!' she said. 'You never ask for anything or offer advice. You never state an opinion, even though you've certainly got one!'

Elisabeth's eyes seemed lost in the far distance. They had that inward look that had frightened Katarina when she was a child.

She tried to control herself, but failed. 'You call it "respecting others" when you won't get involved or refuse to confide in me. How did you think I felt last night when you were going on about your love affairs and the abortion?' she snapped.

Elisabeth was as pale as Katarina was flushed. 'Our behaviour patterns are handed down to us and we accept or reject them. My mother wanted to know everything about me – she had to. It was how she survived.'

'I know – I knew her too. She sucked her children dry – you and your brothers. Not to mention Olof.'

'That's where you're wrong,' Elisabeth said. She was crying.

This was dreadful. Katarina's conscience pricked. She crossed the kitchen and put her arm round her mother's shoulders.

Elisabeth blew her nose on a piece of kitchen towel.

Katarina sat down and, for a time, neither woman spoke.

Finally, Elisabeth said, 'Let's give it a try. I'll rent the flat from you and move in just after Christmas. Then I can help you when the baby arrives. We'll give it a year and then we'll see.'

'Are you going to keep the Gävle flat?'

'Yes, but I'll let it.'

Elisabeth had many friends in Gävle and was active in several societies and study groups. She was sometimes asked to lecture on her work. When Katarina thought about it she realized that her mother was an important figure in her home town and had a lot to lose by moving. She was taken aback: she had not considered that her mother had a life of her own. Ashamed, she said, 'Of course you mustn't move, Mama. I'll be fine.'

'Don't be silly, my dear. Besides, I want to mean something to your child. Guess what I was thinking in bed last night.'

'I can't.'

'That my decision to go for early retirement was a sign from God.'

'Thus spake the clergyman's daughter,' Katarina said, and Elisabeth smiled.

Practical things filled the rest of the day. They had to empty the water tank and drain the pipes, tidy the house, set the rat-traps, fit the double-glazing and tape over the gaps around the window-frames, clear out the larder, defrost the fridge and the deep-freeze. They would leave the cottage together. Elisabeth would return to Gävle for her last term as a teacher and Katarina was going to Stockholm. She had to talk to Jack.

'I'm frightened about that,' she said.

'He's a reasonable man, surely.'

'Is he? This morning I felt as if I hardly knew him.'

It was warm enough to have lunch outside before they left. When they were having coffee afterwards, Katarina asked, 'Mama, do you believe in love?'

'Love? The great romantic . . . ?'

'Yes.'

'I don't know. I've never experienced it,' Elisabeth said. 'You know more about it than I do. You've been in love so many times.'

'I certainly know a lot about being in love.' She laughed. 'So, you fall in love. The blood rushes to your head. Music's playing, the birds are singing. It's a very physical sensation. It's wonderful.'

'It sounds rather selfish.'

'No, it isn't. It's about his skin against yours, an exploration of a body that's not yours. A man's body, so different from your own. Your eyes look deep into his eyes, your mouths join. It isn't selfish, it's the opposite. You surrender yourself. There's a kind of madness about it, but it's wonderful. "Love" has to be kept out of it – or at any rate what goes with great love, the promises, pressures, complications and demands.'

Elisabeth laughed too now, but even so Katarina hesitated before she dared to say, 'It's been different with Jack. The first moment we met, I felt I knew him. Which was strange, you know, because he's a foreigner. He seemed to confirm all the stereotypes about Americans. He's open and direct in a way that makes a half-truth sound more plausible than the whole truth. And the way he moves is pure Hollywood, as you know. Even so . . .' Katarina gazed unseeingly into the forest. She sounded surprised when she continued, 'It's weird. When we stood there looking into each other's eyes, I felt I'd known him all my life.' She closed her eyes and recalled the dull party, their handshake, his chat-up line: 'So, I've made it. I've met a Beautiful Swedish Woman.'

It was time to leave. The sun had passed its zenith and was sinking slowly towards the mountain range in the west.

They had to go.

For a long time, they stood in the yard looking at each other, before they walked to their cars.

5

When Katarina reached the E4 motorway at the Uppsala slip-road, she recalled what Jack had said to her on the journey back from that Gävle visit: 'Most people resent their mothers, maybe because of some characteristic, or even a habit, but you don't, do you?'

She had taken her time to answer him. 'Actually, I do. When I was in my teens, I argued with her all the time but even now she can make me furious. What really gets to me is the way she's right all the time.' Then she had laughed – genuinely: something amusing had occurred to her. 'Often I'm irritated by the way she uses words. Her carefully thought-out, well-formulated sentences. Her inexhaustible knowledge of everything – society, history, religion, psychology, whatever. It makes me tired so I scream at her. Part of me reverts to childhood. She knows it and I do too. Sooner or later we laugh about it together.'

Jack had shaken his head and stayed silent as they drove past the lights at the Uppsala junction. Then he said reluctantly, 'My mother's speech – her language – was the opposite. She didn't spell things out, she expected me to understand what she meant as a kind of subtext. That is all very well in a certain kind of novel, but it's horrible in real life. Especially for a child who's struggling to please.'

'I know just what you mean. My grandmother was a "lady". That's how she put it. What it really meant was that she was deeply inhibited, especially when it came to love and sex. The idea seemed to be that respectable women were indifferent to sex.' She had sighed. 'What she was trying to say was that my grandfather had taken her against her will. He was far from the seductive type.' Her voice had been sad but now she sounded angry: 'She focused her passions on her child. She smothered Elisabeth, watching over, scrutinizing her every thought and feeling. It was called maternal love, but seemed more like imprisonment.'

At that point they had joined the motorway to Stockholm. He put his foot down and drove far too fast, his hands gripping the steering-wheel so hard that his knuckles turned white.

She felt ashamed then – she had spoken like her mother, too freely and impressively.

That had happened in May. Now it was late September. When she had twisted and turned through Norrtull and joined the southbound traffic in the tunnel, it struck her suddenly how much of the conversation she remembered from that Gävle visit, what had been said during the evening with her mother, and that rather unpleasant exchange in the car on the way back. She had always found memories hard to bring to the surface and had thought of them as lost, like treasure-chests on the ocean floor. At times she had grieved about her failure to remember and thought that people without memories lacked depth.

She had a recurring dream: she was diving through dark water towards treasure-chests half buried in the sand at the bottom of the sea. They were heavy and had strong locks, which she could not force. Then she was swimming strongly towards the surface, reached it and filled her lungs with air. She could wash the sand out of her hair, float and allow herself to be carried by the waves. The sun, the wind, the open sea, all that was pure pleasure.

She would wake strangely sad but her reaction was always the same: she was glad that the chests had been locked.

6

She put away the car in the garage, feeling uneasy, as she always did when she had to confront something difficult. She unlocked the door and saw his coat, thrown on the shelf in the hall. Jack was stretched out in an armchair in the sitting room. He leapt up when she came in. 'At last! There you are.'

Oh, damn, she thought. As they held each other, she thought that all would be well after they had talked.

Then she saw that he was upset, even a little shaky. 'I need a drink,' he said. 'A big one.'

Katarina fetched the whisky, poured him a large one and a little for herself.

He emptied his glass in one gulp. Then he said, 'My mother is ill. Cancer. Or so they say.'

'Jack, that's awful. I'm so sorry. Is she in hospital?'

'Yes, she is. On a drip, whatever.'

'Oh, my God . . . you must go to her.'

'Of course. I've got a seat on a plane leaving Frankfurt tomorrow morning for LA.'

'Have you spoken to her doctor?'

'No. Just my sister and . . .'

'And?'

'She said that Mom won't die until she's seen me.'

He noticed the dark clouds drifting across Katarina's face, saw her eyes narrow. 'Surely you've talked to your wife?' she asked.

'There's no point. She'll just say what she's always been saying, which is that Mom's playing to the gallery, manipulating me. As ever.'

He held out his glass and she poured him another drink. 'They didn't like each other much, Mom and Grace,' he added.

Katarina was silent. She felt uncomfortable, asking him questions. All she said was: 'We know so little about each other, you and I.'

He smiled. 'But that's what's wonderful about us, real magic. No digging for secrets, no demands.'

Rage flooded Katarina. It was as if flames were burning inside her. She tried to control herself, breathing slowly, ignoring the piston-like pounding of her heart. Keep cool, she told herself. And say nothing.

But she couldn't. Instead she heard herself say, 'Jack, our "magic" relationship has changed. I'm pregnant.'

Seconds passed. Then he straightened, took a few steps towards her and asked harshly, 'How did it happen?'

'I forgot my pill.'

'*Forgot!*' he yelled. 'Get rid of it! Christ almighty, abortion's easy enough to come by in this mother-fucking socialist country.'

'No,' she said.

He was still shouting: 'You'd have anyone with a cock! Everyone knows you're a whore. You change men the way other women change their panties.'

She stayed silent. She knew that he knew the baby was his.

He took a step forward, coming very close to her. Then he hit her, his fist striking her left ear. He struck once more, her nose this time. I mustn't faint, she thought. I mustn't faint. Blood was gushing from her nose as she staggered towards the bathroom door. She locked herself in, found a big towel and tried to stop it. Her ear hurt so much that she sank down on the toilet seat. Strange images floated in front of her eyes. He was banging on the door now. 'Open up, for fuck's sake. You whoring bitch!'

The bathroom was whirling around Katarina.

She found the strength to pull herself together. 'Jack,' she said, managing to keep her voice steady, 'I have my mobile in my pocket. If you don't get out of my home *now* I'll phone the police. Violence towards women is illegal in this mother-fucking socialist country. The police will stop you at the airport if you try to leave.'

Silence outside the bathroom door. Then he shouted, 'How much do you want? I'll pay, sure. No problem, I'll pay in dollars.'

'*Go away.*'

At last she heard the front door slam and staggered out into the hall, locked the door and fastened the safety-chain.

The pain in her ear was terrible.

Elisabeth let the telephone ring and ring but no one answered. They might have gone out for a meal, she said to herself. But Katarina had promised to phone her and she usually kept her word.

Suddenly Elisabeth felt anxious, and then, illogically, frightened. It was ten o'clock at night and it would take her at least three hours to drive to Katarina's. Olof, she thought. I must get hold of Olof. He's only in Uppsala.

He answered, thank God. 'Something's happened to Katarina!' she shouted. 'Please, please, do something. You've got keys!'

'Take it easy, Mama. I'm leaving now.'

Less than an hour later Olof pressed Katarina's bell. No one came to the door, but he could see through the letter-box that the light was on in the hall. He unlocked the door, but the safety-chain was on. He hammered on the panel. After a while he heard her shout: 'Go to hell! I never, never . . .'

Her voice faded. He flapped the letter-box, and called, 'It's me! Olof! Can you hear me?'

Ten minutes later he was wiping the blood off her face. She was shaking and icy cold, so he wrapped her in blankets. The trembling did not stop.

He called the ambulance and was told that it would be with him in a quarter of an hour. While he was waiting, he telephoned Elisabeth: 'Katarina has been involved in . . . well, she's been hurt. I'm waiting for the ambulance to take her to the Southern General Hospital. I'll call you again as soon as I can. Go to bed now and try to sleep.'

Olof was sitting in the hospital waiting area, reviewing various different ways of murdering the American when a doctor came to see him. Katarina had a broken eardrum and damage to the auditory canal. 'Who are you?' he asked.

Olof heard the suspicion in the man's voice. 'Her brother.'

The doctor looked sceptical, but Olof told him that their mother, worried that she had not heard from her daughter, had called and asked him to check on her. In the end the hospital staff believed him, but he had to show proof of his identity. Later a nurse brought him coffee and a cinnamon bun.

The hours passed. The doctor returned and said that he hoped they had saved her hearing, but she had to stay overnight. 'You might as well go home now. You can always pray for her – after all, you're a clergyman.' The sarcasm was unmistakable but Olof only smiled. He was used to that kind of thing.

'However, she has been attacked,' the doctor went on, 'and I shall have to report it. Do you know who her assailant was?'

'Only that he's an American.'

'No name?'

'Unfortunately not. Our mother knows, though. I've just spoken to her on the phone and she's on her way here. I'll stay until she arrives, if I may.'

They let him lie down on a trolley in Katarina's room. He slept uneasily and woke every time she moved. In the middle of the night she once said, sounding surprised, 'Olof! What are you doing here?'

He did not answer but went to her bedside and took her hand in his. She closed her eyes and whispered, 'I'm trying to remember what happened.'

After a while, she opened her eyes and said, 'Olof, I'm so ashamed.'

He said nothing – otherwise he would have bellowed that it was Jack, the violent bastard, who should bloody well be ashamed.

After a while Katarina said, 'You see, I'm crazy about him.'

'Crazy love is often a sign that one . . . somehow recognizes the other – as a reflection of oneself. One aspect of a deeply divided self.'

Katarina looked startled. Light seemed to flicker among the dark shadows in her face. 'Sleep well, big sister,' he whispered to her.

At dawn Elisabeth arrived, her eyes bloodshot after the long drive in the dark. The doctor came to speak to her. He had been on night duty and his eyes were as red as hers. 'I need to know the name of the American,' he said.

Elisabeth told him, and that he was a visiting lecturer at the University of Stockholm. 'I don't have his address, though, neither here nor in California.'

'The police can get that information from the university.'

Before the doctor's report reached the police, Jack's plane had taken off from Arlanda airport. It was of no consequence. Katarina refused to allow her attacker to be charged.

7

They went to Katarina's flat, at Åsö Street. At once Elisabeth started clearing up. There were bloodstains on the carpet in the sitting room and dried blood on the hall floor. The coat-stand in the hall had fallen over and the coats were scattered about. An empty whisky bottle stood on the sitting-room table.

'Does he drink?'

'Yes.'

They exchanged a glance.

Katarina crawled into bed and fell asleep at once.

Olof was sitting at the desk in the study, talking on the telephone to Erika, who sighed with relief when she heard that Katarina's hearing would probably return. Then she said, quite sharply, 'When you phoned from the hospital you said that the American had been waiting for Katarina in her flat. He must have keys.'

Olof should have prayed to his God. Instead he swore.

Elisabeth systematically searched every item of clothing in the hall for spare keys. Then she went through the desk, the bookshelves, the kitchen drawers.

'We've got to get her away from here,' Olof said.

'Let's rest for a couple of hours first,' Elisabeth replied. And so they did: they slept, then made some sandwiches.

Later they tucked Katarina into the back of Olof's big Volvo and set out for Uppsala, where Erika was waiting with a hot supper. Elisabeth followed in her own car.

Katarina stood in the hall, holding Erika's hands. She did not want to have to depend on her sister-in-law – she thought of her, a Sami woman, as rather fey. But Erika seemed infinitely wise. She had realized that the injuries would make chewing painful and gave Katarina her soup in a baby's bottle.

How typical of Erika, Elisabeth thought, as she tried to angle the teat correctly in Katarina's mouth. 'I'm out of practice. It's a long time since I had to do this,' Erika said, her voice oddly thick.

After supper Katarina closed her eyes. Sleep was all she wanted.

Suddenly, two little boys materialized, one at either side of her bed. The older one whispered, 'Can we pat your cheek?'

'Please, just my hands,' she whispered, and felt them stroking her wrists and arms.

'That car driver, was he drunk?'

'Yes, he was. Drunk and mad.'

'He didn't know what he was doing,' Sam said.

'No, he didn't.'

'But you'll be well again soon, Papa says.'

'Oh, yes, of course I will.'

'We'll draw some stories, then.'

'I promise.'

She opened her eyes and looked at the children. How pretty they were.

They were on their way out but stopped in the doorway, turned and waved to her.

She could not sleep. Strangely lucid images from her time with Jack kept coming into her mind.

An episode during their summer of sailing in the archipelago. They had dropped anchor and gone to sit on deck in their anoraks. It was windy, and the rigging was singing.

He had asked her about Olof and his family. 'What kind of relationship do you have with your brother?'

She replied without having to think, 'We've always been friends, close friends. We like each other wholeheartedly.'

'But he's a clergyman. Surely he's got something to say about all your men.'

'Why should he?'

'Doesn't he know?'

'Of course he does. I've always been able to talk to him about everything. Actually, I can say much more to him than . . . to Mama.'

In her mind's eye, she could see Jack's astonished face.

'Listen, Jack, Olof doesn't see himself as a shepherd and his fellow man as a lost sheep that must be captured and dragged back into flock.'

'What kind of priest is he, then?'

'The kind that respects every human being, and the choices he or she has made on their way through life.'

Jack had been shaking his head. He did not understand all this. After a while he had said, 'I had this idea that Christianity entreated people to keep to the straight and narrow path.'

'What an ungenerous view of it. Surely you, more than most, should know that religion is about much more than that.'

They had shared a tin of ham and a bottle of wine in silence.

But once they had crawled into their sleeping-bags he had returned to the theme. 'So, what's his wife like?'

Katarina had giggled and said that, as with most things, the answer was not straightforward. 'You see, Erika embodies everything you'd think a clergyman's wife should be. She bakes bread, does housework without a murmur, invites members of the congregation to coffee after church and listens to old folk talk about their ailments.' Then she laughed. 'She couldn't be more right for the job. Even her looks fit the bill – she's a bit of an earth-mother. She's plump, with warm, brown eyes. And yet – well, she's the most amazing person I've ever met. Completely unpredictable.'

'In what way?'

'You never know how she'll react. Whose side she's going to be on. Without any warning, in the middle of an ordinary conversation, she'll say the most extraordinary things, in her mild, reasonable voice. Things that turn your preconceptions inside out. She may be a housewife and mother but she's highly intelligent too.

And intuitive, so much so it's almost spooky at times. She sometimes sounds as if she can see far into the distance, through mists and walls.'

'You sound weird when you talk about her – because you don't like her, I guess.'

'I'm jealous of her,' Katarina confessed.

'Because she's got your brother?'

'No, because she and Mama are such friends. They're very close.'

Now, she heard herself say that again, and her voice sounded like a child's. Had Jack heard that note too? Probably. He had sounded happier when he asked, 'You said they've got two little boys?'

'Yes, they're lovely kids.'

She told him of how for years Erika and Olof could not conceive. There had been endless medical investigations, then several attempts at engineering a pregnancy and, finally, despair. There was something wrong with Erika and she would never be able to have children. It was a cruel blow to someone who had longed all her life for children. Erika had become depressed and gone into therapy.

She had even suggested divorce. 'Olof would be a perfect father,' she had said to Elisabeth once, when they were at her cottage by the river Ljusnan. They had spent a few nights there, and in the end they accepted Elisabeth's firm, repeated advice. Adopt, she said.

Both Olof and Erika had contacts in Vietnam. Eventually, after a long wait and much arguing with bureaucracy in Sweden and Vietnam, they were allowed to travel to Hanoi and collect their children. 'Sweet babies, such beautiful boys,' Katarina had said, and her voice had held a new note of pure joy.

Jack had propped himself on his elbow in the bunk. 'Hey, does this mean your nephews are Chinese?' he asked.

'Chinese? Are the Vietnamese actually Chinese?'

In the little cabin, she had not noticed the distance in his voice.

She went on talking about the boys, how charming they were, how talented and clever. 'So incredibly smart.'

He had said that the Chinese were often smart, quick on the uptake . . .

Had he used the word 'calculating'? She could not remember, but as she lay in her bed in the Uppsala manse, she thought that she had failed to notice quite a few warning signs of how Jack's mind worked.

What had Olof said? 'A reflection of one aspect of the divided self?' She did not understand and did not want to.

Her ear was aching badly now and she took a painkiller.

Then she slept.

8

Jack had put his seat to recline in the plane, but he still could not sleep. He needed another whisky, but he had had two already since leaving Frankfurt and he felt embarrassed to order another.

The plane was flying into the light.

Christ, she was so beautiful. Long, long legs, the muscles moving under her tanned skin. Round buttocks and firm, full breasts. When he had seen her walking naked along the beach, he had been reminded of figures sculpted by ancient masters, with her perfect poise, the way her head balanced on her slender neck. And then her face with the frank eyes, deep blue like the sky on late summer evenings. Her mobile mouth, changing with her shifting moods – how easily it became demanding, wanting to taste his body. His cock.

He had been shocked at first, but she laughed at him. 'You Americans! So puritan.'

Those summer nights when they had finally fallen asleep in the warm cabin, he had thought often that he had never before understood what erotic pleasure meant. That, in spite of his many affairs and long marriage.

She liberated me.

What that would mean now, he did not even dare to wonder. Instead he wept.

When the stewardess passed, he whispered his order and gratefully drank the double shot as if it had been water. Then he could escape the memory of how it had ended, his and Katarina's love affair.

He would never think about it.

Later he woke, took some paracetamol and decided to concentrate on Grace. He remembered their first meeting, their wedding and their first year together in their new home. How good everything had been.

His supervisor at the university, a man who had looked after his postgraduates well, had had two daughters, of whom Grace was one. Jack had met them both at a party in his professor's house. The younger girl was pretty but dull. Grace, the elder, seemed shy and sad, but melancholic women had always aroused him. He fell in love, eager to comfort her, and convinced that he could.

Grace's eyes had been frightened. They were huge and almost black. Sadness had already drawn bitter lines around her mouth.

Her parents had tried to warn him off. Grace, they told him, had suffered since her early teens from depression. He ignored them, made some naïve remark about love and its power to set the spirit free.

In the beginning it seemed to work. They had bought a house together. She decorated it and went to cooking classes. When she felt down, he was there for her and did what he could. He made sure he was a considerate lover, and gave her presents, jewellery or pretty underwear. He enjoyed his power and was happy.

Then their first child was born, a son. His mother-in-law cared for the baby. Grace was in hospital with post-natal depression, or so they told him. When she came home, vague with medication, he gave her roses. He had cooked a welcome-home meal and, in bed afterwards, she gave herself to him.

She became pregnant again. This time she was calm and full of confidence, but when she came home with their second baby boy, the darkness had closed around her again. Jack found a nanny, but the older child was happy with his grandmother. Then they discovered that the baby was damaged. Learning difficulties were diagnosed.

Jack was away a lot, doing fieldwork for his doctoral thesis. When he came home Grace was profoundly withdrawn. He watched her sinking, sinking. He tried to talk to her, and caressed her, but failed to reach her. Those were the times when he shook her, then hit her. Afterwards he escaped abroad on long engagements.

★

He phoned his sister from the airport in Los Angeles. She told him that their mother had left hospital and was at home. She did not have cancer. Her alarming physical symptoms had been caused by depression. 'She'll be OK now. Just hurry up and come home.'

His connecting flight to San José was waiting. When he arrived he hired a car. As he walked to pick it up, his legs seemed out of control. Jet-legs, he said to himself, then remembered how much he had drunk and drove carefully.

He should be in despair over Katarina, he thought. He should be furious with his mother, who Grace had told him was 'acting up'. But he was beyond emotion.

It took him the best part of an hour to drive to one of Berkeley's smartest suburbs. Then he saw it, his childhood home at the top of the hill: a spacious, glamorous villa surrounded by magnificent park-like grounds with a swimming-pool. *The American way of life.*

He had always been unhappy there, a frightened child tied to his mother. His father had hit her, and to this day he hated him. He had not seen his father for twenty years. Christ, how he hated him. And what beatings he'd taken as a boy. Christ almighty.

His sister Evelyn came to meet him. She had lost weight and looked more drawn than he remembered. She smiled at him, though, and they held each other in an awkward embrace.

His mother, wearing a blue robe, was lying on one of the white sofas in the large drawing room. She stretched out her arms to him and he hugged her. Perhaps he had never truly loved anyone but her. They said little. A few pretty tears came to her eyes and she smiled the familiar smile, which did not crease her cheeks.

She looked younger than her daughter. 'You must be exhausted,' she said.

'I sure am.'

'Your room is ready. Why don't you take a bath and go to bed?' Evelyn said.

Their mother nodded, but insisted that they must drink to Jack's homecoming first. The housekeeper, who had served the family for a long time, came in with a tray of champagne and glasses. Her back was bent now, and her hands were shaking. Jack greeted her and, to his surprise, realized he felt ashamed in front of her.

When they went upstairs, Jack said to his sister, 'Is there a bottle of whisky?'

'It's already in your room.'

He slept for ten hours.

It was at breakfast the next day that his mother told him, in passing, that Grace has filed for divorce and had gone away with the children, leaving no address.

Late that night, when he calculated that it would be morning in Stockholm, Jack rang Katarina on his mobile, so his mother could not eavesdrop.

A man answered. Jack asked to speak to Katarina.

'Who's speaking?' The voice at the other end was guarded.

'Jack O'Hara.'

The man's voice cracked. 'You bastard! And you have the nerve to phone her!'

'I want to talk to Katarina.'

Now the voice was under control and very cold. 'Katarina is still unconscious most of the time. She's had an operation for extensive head injuries, including a fractured jaw and damage to the auditory canal. She will probably . . . never fully recover.'

'Christ . . . oh, Jesus Christ, help me.'

The icy voice went on relentlessly, 'You're wanted here for attempted murder. The police have your photograph and passport number. Whatever you do, don't come to this country. And you might as well throw away your keys to her flat. I'm about to fit a new lock.'

The receiver was slammed down.

Jack staggered to bed and opened the whisky bottle. It occurred to him that unlike Grace, who had tried to get out of his way, Katarina had just stood there, contemptuous. The arrogant Swedish bitch had been too proud for her own good.

He loved her so fucking much.

When his mother came to say goodnight, he had already drunk himself unconscious.

9

One night Katarina was woken by a storm. The wind was howling across the bare fields surrounding the city and gusting against the windows. Dead branches were torn off old trees and crashed on to the roof.

Nothing bad would happen, though: her mother was sleeping peacefully in a folding bed next to hers.

Then Katarina made a discovery. She could hear the sound of the storm, the wind rushing through the trees, the creaking branches . . . She could hear! Her ear no longer hurt. Cautiously, to avoid waking Elisabeth, she sat on the edge of her bed and plugged her good ear with her thumb. Her left ear picked up sounds, a little muffled and difficult to distinguish, but she could hear. And the pain was gone.

She wanted to go back to sleep then, but could not. I cannot escape it now, she thought. It is terrible, but I must face it.

It was four o'clock in the morning. The thoughts she had dreaded were pursuing each other in her mind, one stumbling over the next. She felt ashamed, furious, frightened as the images of what had happened came back to her.

She could remember who had said what. The abusive words he had shouted at her. The blows to her head. Who was he – who was he really? she asked herself.

It was almost dawn when she dozed off. Sleeping lightly, near the edge of consciousness, she dreamed of a breaking wave, as high as a house, coming towards her. At first she was standing on the beach, but then she was running for her life. She tore across the sandy beach and clambered up the rocks. Up and up, until she reached a point from where she could watch the wave crash on to the land, disintegrate, and vanish back into the sea, where another huge wave was forming.

There must be an earthquake at the bottom of the sea, she

thought. The next moment she was wide awake. Elisabeth was sitting up in her bed, watching her.

'I was dreaming about a storm,' Katarina said.

'Seems reasonable. The wind was really up tonight.'

'Mama, I've got to tell you. I can hear the wind with my left ear.'

Elisabeth's eyes widened. 'Are you sure?' She did a series of tests to check Katarina's hearing: first she held her hand over her daughter's good ear, then a pillow. The girl could hear! No doubt about it. Elisabeth's eyes overflowed with tears of joy.

Olof came to see her, then the boys slipped in and held her hands. Olof phoned the doctor, who promised to call later that morning. Before he hung up, the doctor said, 'It seems to be resolving itself as we hoped.'

Elisabeth had to return to Gävle, where she was scheduled to lecture that afternoon.

'You must go, Mama, don't worry about me,' Katarina said, as tears streamed down her cheeks.

'It's just like when you were little and I had to go to work. I knew you minded, but you were always so self-contained – for my sake. But when you were waving to me through the window, I could see that you were crying too.'

Suddenly, Katarina could do lots of things that had been impossible. She could chew a liver pâté sandwich. She could help with the washing-up and almost laughed when Jon asked why her face was blue and yellow. She could shower and get dressed. All of that was wonderful. Erika helped her with her hair, which was long and newly washed.

'The worst thing is the shame,' Katarina said.

Unlike Olof, Erika did not tell her that it was Jack who should be ashamed. Instead she said, 'I think . . . I know what you mean. I believe all abused women feel ashamed.'

'That's crazy.'

'Well, yes. But it has nothing to do with reason.'

Katarina felt cold. Erika sat her in an armchair in front of the big wood-burning stove and got a fire going. 'Would you like a cup of coffee?'

'Yes, please.'

Katarina looked around the sitting room. She liked it very much. It was modest, worn but beautiful.

The two little boys padded in to her. Jon almost whispered when he asked, 'Now that you're well again, can you draw a story?'

One Christmas, when Elisabeth had told them a story, Katarina drew it, one picture after another, following the tale as it developed. The boys had clung to her chair, breathing heavily, sighing and shrieking with excitement as the images grew and changed before their eyes. It had become a family tradition.

Later, Katarina had continued illustrating stories when she and the boys were together on their own. Her tales were not as colourful as Elisabeth's, but her pictures had greater depth when she drew at her own pace.

Now the boys were standing together, their heads to the side, imploring. They were irresistible. 'I'll try. Fetch me the crayons, please, and the big drawing pad.'

Erika came in with the coffee just as the boys got back. 'Are you strong enough to do this?' she asked.

'I'd like to try.'

Katarina sipped her coffee and stared at the blank sheet of paper in front of her. She picked up a crayon . . . but her head was empty.

Then she remembered her dream. A big wave, threatening her life. Suddenly she realized that it was another part of the old dream about treasure-chests buried in mud at the bottom of the sea.

'Once upon a time there was a little girl who lived in a house by the sea. She walked on the beach every day and listened to the ocean. It was singing to her, a song without end about the huge depths of the ocean. She loved that song.'

The sea grew on the paper. It was blue like the sky but

shimmered like gold. The girl was standing on a white beach, a tiny figure against the expanse of water, with a rocky slope in the background.

'The girl collected secrets, the most secret things ever, and she wanted nobody to find out about them. She was determined to keep them safe, so she decided one day to hide her secrets in the sea. She had worked out what she must do.

'You see, she not only collected secrets, she saved boxes too. Nice, strong boxes, each with its own lock and key. One day she took her secrets and put one into each box. Afterwards she went up into the attic and found a big chest. It was heavy and had double locks. Of course, she had to do this at night while her mother was asleep.'

Katarina drew a picture of the girl struggling down a steep staircase, dragging a chest behind her. Then, another scene: the girl sitting outside the house, putting lots of small boxes into the chest.

'It was a summer's night and there was a full moon.' Katarina drew a huge moon. 'She wanted to take the chest far out at sea and let it sink down into the depths.'

'What did she do?'

Katarina thought for a while and then she told them, 'She borrowed a boat. A rowing-boat was tied to the pier down by the beach.'

In her next drawing, the heavy chest was in the boat and the girl was rowing. Then, she had rowed so far away that she was just a tiny dot on the horizon. There, she pushed the chest overboard. Katarina drew a splash as it hit the water. By now she felt tired and a little dizzy.

But the boys were shouting, 'What happened next? Tell us!'

'It's a sad story,' Katarina said. By now her eyes and Erika's were locked together.

'Why is it sad?' Sam asked.

Katarina remembered that he loved sad stories. She drew breath and said, 'As time went past, the girl longed to see her secrets again. She wanted to get them back because she couldn't remember what they were. So she took it into her head to swim straight out into the sea and dive down to find her chest.'

She drew the girl swimming towards the horizon. In the next picture, she dived down through the deep water to the chest, which was half buried in the sand at the bottom of the sea. They could see that the chest was securely locked.

'Then, you see, the girl needed air,' Katarina said. 'She had to be quick. Once she was up at the surface again, she felt happy. She rinsed the sand from her hair, then lay down on her back to float for a while and enjoy the sunshine.'

She drew the girl floating in the sea, the waves carrying her in towards the beach.

'My arm is tired now.'

Erika poured her some coffee, stroked her hair and said, 'It's time for you to rest.'

But the boys were protesting, 'We've got to know what happened!'

So Katarina went on. 'One night, there was a wild storm and the girl woke because of the din the waves made when they hit the beach. The waves were as high as . . . skyscrapers. They reached all the way up to the house where the girl and her family lived.'

She drew a tiny house. The girl, her mother, her grandfather, grandmother and all her brothers were running towards the rocks. They clambered on to the highest.

'Then her mother told the girl that there was an earthquake at the bottom of the sea. The girl started crying, because she realized that her treasure-chest might be smashed to bits. Then her secrets would float in to land along the coast.'

'She has to go out looking for them,' Jon said.

'But the coast's very, very long and it's got a thousand inlets and a hundred thousand sharp stones.'

'She's got to look for a long time.'

'But her feet would get sore.' Katarina drew the girl's small feet with big, bleeding wounds.

'That's silly,' Jon said. 'She should wear proper shoes.'

'Katarina is tired now and has to rest,' Erika said, firmly.

The boys knew they must do as they were told but before they said goodbye and left the room, they both shouted that later they wanted to hear the end of the story.

'A story has to have an end, doesn't it?' Jon asked.

'Well, yes, I hope so,' Katarina replied.

10

The family doctor was called Lasse Simonsson. He had visited Katarina on her first day in hospital. Now he had her file and some instructions from her consultant. He turned up later that afternoon to examine her hearing. As he conducted his tests, his smile grew broader, and eventually he said, 'You'll soon be up and about. Still, you must take care to avoid loud noises and you can't drive for a while.' He signed her off work for a month.

'No, no, I have to go back to work!' Katrina protested.

'Do you really want to put your hearing at risk?'

Katarina burst into tears. She had counted on work as her escape route.

She was even more upset when he said, 'I must advise you against returning to your flat.'

'Why do you say that?'

'It's far too noisy for you to be in the centre of town.'

'But I can't just hang about here . . . for ever.'

'Of course you can, you know that,' Erika sounded almost angry.

'Your sister-in-law is one of those people who find it hard to accept help,' the doctor said to Erika.

'Fancies himself as a shrink,' Erika hissed, after he had gone. Katarina had to smile.

Olof came home for supper. The whole family ate early, at about five in the afternoon. They told him what the doctor had said and he beamed. 'It's lovely to have you here,' he said.

'Stop being so nice or I'll start crying again,' Katarina mumbled.

Olof had an engagement that evening, and when he had gone, Erika gave the boys a bath and tucked them into bed. Katarina did the washing-up in the large, old-fashioned kitchen. I'll give them a dishwasher, she thought.

She discovered something important when she stacked the clean plates a little carelessly in the cupboard: the sharp noises hurt her ear. Dr Simonsson's right, she thought. I've got to be careful.

When the children had gone to sleep Erika said, 'We need some fresh air. Do you think you're fit enough for a walk round the house?'

The idea made Katarina almost happy. Erika pulled a large woollen cap well down over her ears and lent her Olof's large, fur-lined winter anorak and his boots, which caused Katarina to make another discovery. When she bent to pull them on, she felt so dizzy she had to sit down. The hall revolved around her. Erika waited. It was some time before they could go out.

'Somehow, your sense of balance is all bound up with your ears,' Erika said, as they walked ten metres along the street in one direction then back again, slowly. To Katarina, even walking slowly, step by step, felt like an adventure.

When they were back inside, sitting in front of the fire, Erika said 'You need proper shoes to explore that coastline . . . and I know an exceptionally good shoemaker.'

Katarina did not answer at once. Then she swallowed and said, 'I suppose I'm prejudiced – against psychobabble, I mean. But I'd like to tackle this . . . my . . .'

'That's exactly what I thought when I was at my worst. But I was wrong and I did accept help in the end.'

'I remember, you were seeing some specialist counsellor. But it's not as if I . . . have had as hard a time as you did.'

'How do you know?'

'I don't,' Katarina said, and could not stop herself touching her belly with the tiny shoot inside it.

'Think about it.'

Then they decided to watch TV until bed-time.

11

The storm had left Uppland County, and now they had several blazing late-summer days. The sun shone on a golden world.

'Let's spend a day in the forest,' Erika said.

After packing the car with a rug, sandwiches, coffee and cocoa in Thermos flasks, they set off, along roads lined with flame-coloured trees, which twisted and turned between wide fields covered with pale-yellow stubble. Here and there earth mounds covered dolmens in which unknown Viking chiefs slept their thousand-year sleep.

They parked at the edge of the forest road and walked through the piles of red and gold leaves. The boys ran ahead, shouting and kicking up flurries of them. The forest smelt of autumn; a melancholy odour of mushrooms and decay.

Katarina was wearing ear-plugs, but she took them out to listen to the children's laughter and the rustling of the leaves. She caught up with Erika. 'I've decided to walk along that coast alone,' she said. 'On bleeding feet,' she added, with a disarming smile.

'That's fine by me. Let things happen at their own pace.'

'They do, anyway. I hold myself back as much as I can.'

A little later they stopped in front of a huge, berry-laden sloe bush. 'Oh, damn. We should've brought our gloves,' Katarina said.

'Lets go back to the car and fetch them.'

Later, they picked a big bag of the frosted, dark blue berries. Their arms and Katarina's face got scratched.

Jon was watching while Erika washed the scratches with disinfectant and said to Katarina, 'Now you're not just yellow and blue, you've got red bits too.'

'Why did you pick those berries anyway?' Sam shouted, and spat one out. 'They taste horrible.'

'We'll make sloe juice,' Erika told them, and the boys chorused that they would never, ever drink it.

They spread the rug on the ground and settled down to have their picnic. The boys ran about under the trees and into the bushes like small wild things. They brought Katarina an abandoned bird's nest and she had to explain, straw by straw, exactly how the birds had constructed it.

'Which ones lived in it?' Jon whispered.

'I think it must have been pied wagtails.'

'Where are they now?'

'They've moved to Egypt, because it's getting so cold here. And they took their babies with them.'

'I want to go to Egypt. Where is it?'

'Far to the south, where the sun is now,' Erika said. The boys ran off again.

'Hey, it's so far it would take a thousand days to get there,' Erika called after them. They stopped and looked disappointed.

Then Sam said to Jon, 'Come on, we'll pretend.'

'Last night I was lying awake thinking about shame,' Erika said, 'especially what we talked about yesterday, the victim's shame.'

'I know it's irrational but it plagues me every night. Did you find any answers?'

'Only that you're right. You should be ashamed for allowing yourself to be humiliated.'

Silence. The forest itself seemed to hold its breath.

Katarina finally nodded. 'It's true. I did allow it. And I used him, just as I've used other men. Do you see what I mean? I closed my eyes to the kind of man he really was. God knows, there were enough warning signs.'

'Maybe you don't pay enough attention to the warning signs in yourself,' Erika said.

There was no more time to talk, because the boys came running back. They had met a man who had told them that Egypt was so far away you had to go there in a plane.

'That's right. I forgot to say so,' Erika told them.

'You ask your papa. He's been to Egypt,' Katarina said.

Then they packed up their things and went back to the car.

When they were home again, Katarina said she was tired and needed to rest for a while. 'And cry quietly on my own,' she whispered to Erika.

Katarina and Erika did not meet alone together until late evening.

'I'm a bit slow. When you said that I didn't pay enough attention to the warning signs in myself, what did you mean?'

Erika sighed, and thought for quite a long time. Finally she said that she could not talk about this without reference to her faith. 'You must know that everything has a religious dimension,' she said.

'I don't understand,' Katarina said. 'What has God to do with it?'

'As far as I'm concerned, the way towards God begins with one's faith in oneself.'

'That sounds like an American-style exhortation to love thyself!'

Erika noted the scornful tone but went on, with a shrug, 'Not really, no. More like the classical Greek advice to know thyself.'

'That just sounds like words to me.'

'But to me it means being aware of your feelings and drives, understanding them and seeing them for what they are, however disagreeable. Only then do you get an insight into your own capacity for evil, envy and lust for power.'

'That sounds dreadful.'

'It's hard in the beginning. You find you cast a much longer, darker shadow than you ever imagined.' Erika avoided Katarina's eyes.

'My self-confidence is quite sound.'

Erika laughed. 'Self-confidence and self-knowledge are not the same thing.'

Katarina's heart pounded. 'And how do you define self-confidence?'

'It's something like living up to your rose-tinted image of yourself. And functioning well in the roles you've picked.'

This touched Katarina on the raw. Her voice had an edge when she said, 'So, how do I go about acquiring self-knowledge?'

'You must be attentive to yourself, as I said. Somehow be present inside yourself.'

This baffled Katarina. 'When you went into therapy it helped you to see . . . ?'

'Yes, it did. Children learn early what shame is about – "Naughty, naughty, you should be ashamed of yourself," and, much worse, "Now you've made Mama so sad . . ."' Erika seemed to withdraw into herself to think for a while. Then she said, 'Children are always looking for explanations. If none are forthcoming, they take on the guilt and the shame: "It's my fault that Mama and Papa are having rows, that Papa is shouting, that Mama is crying, that my little brother has a tummy ache." You know what I mean.'

Silence. Erika continued hesitantly, 'One thing I learnt in therapy was that so many of my decisions were made by a childlike me. A childish child, operating at a primitive level of understanding.'

They had switched off the overhead lights and sat together by the flickering fire.

'I know just what you mean,' Katarina said. 'It was my fault that my father hit my mother – because I saw it as my responsibility to protect her . . .' Her voice broke. 'And now I'm confusing her with a repetition of her trauma. Have you realized how she feels about this episode with Jack?'

Erika did not answer.

When they were preparing breakfast the next morning, Katarina asked, 'How do you learn to pay attention to yourself?'

Erika stared at her wide-eyed, then said, 'Get me some coffee first.'

With a mug at hand, she started to search sleepily for the right words. 'Emotions turn up, strong and often unpleasant. Question:

where do they come from? Once I began to look seriously for the answer, I realized that the emotions were related to my self-image. Or, rather, to some hurt or other that had shaken it.

'I need more coffee,' she said suddenly.

Katarina topped up her mug. 'Go on – please.'

'The first self I found was the honest, kindly me, always there for everybody and always keen to please,' Erika said. 'I got to dislike that woman very much, but she kept poking her nose in. Just wouldn't go away. I discovered that she harboured appalling emotions. And her thoughts were unspeakably malicious.'

'I don't understand, Erika. What sort of thoughts?'

In the silence that followed, Katarina saw to her surprise that Erika was blushing up to her hairline.

'Well, let me just give you one example,' she said finally, and after a short pause, 'You and Elisabeth came for dinner with us and I had taken a lot of trouble to prepare a proper three-course meal. Elisabeth said, in passing, that it was lovely and thanked me. Then you two were away again, deep into one of your interminable intellectual exercises. I got on with the dishes and next, looking all smart and lovely, you're floating politely into the kitchen to ask, not as if you mean it, "Can I help at all?" I shake my head, of course, and tell you that I'll come through soon with the coffee. I did the saucepans then, scrubbed them and took a knife to the burnt-on bits. I cut and I scraped and I carved out your self-assured, provocative blue eyes.'

Now Katarina's eyes were round with surprise: 'I remember that evening and how you pushed me out of your kitchen. I decided you enjoyed martyrdom and that I shouldn't try to take away your pleasure.'

'Maybe you weren't far wrong.' Erika laughed.

At that moment, Olof came into the kitchen. 'There's tension in the air,' he said, and poured milk on to his cereal.

'Is there?' Katarina almost screamed at him. 'How astute! Have you ever thought of how you were allowed to be a child while I had to grow up? At the age of six?'

'Yes, I have,' Olof replied. 'I was always aware of it. Sometimes I've wondered if that's why I feel guilty . . . why I feel I have to make up for it somehow.'

The boys were on their way down for breakfast, so Katarina lowered her voice to hiss: 'Fuck off! I don't need anything from you.'

When Katarina ran upstairs, she heard Erika laugh.

Then she hated her sister-in-law.

12

Sleep had always been merciful to Katarina. Now she slept like a child, with the duvet pulled over her head, curled up like a foetus with one hand on her stomach.

Somewhere far away she heard the sounds of a door opening and two little voices murmuring, 'She's asleep.'

Then they were gone.

Still, the children had moved her consciousness to another level, and she was in a frighteningly distinct dream.

She was a child, and had retreated into a corner of a large compartment in a train. Opposite her sat a woman with a little boy asleep in her arms. The woman had tried to hide her damaged face behind a big black scarf, but the blood seeping from her nose and her swollen cheeks were there for all to see. The girl in the corner wanted to comfort her, make her better and call out to her, 'I love you, Mama.' But she realized quickly that she could not cry out. She could not even speak. It was odd, because she could hear. The wheels thumped across the junctions between the rails and glasses rattled in the rack above her seat. She was thirsty, but she could neither reach the water carafe nor ask for a drink.

The most horrible thing was not the train sounds but the ghost-like figures wandering past in the corridor. They would stop and stare. Some shook their heads in compassion, others laughed and a few gloated. She recognized them all, for they came from her home village.

Then the train was braking and she saw her grandfather standing on the platform, his arms reaching out towards her. She could not move. It was as though she had turned to stone. Her mother left, carrying Olof, but the girl had to stay behind. The train rushed northwards in the dark, dunkety-dunkety-dunk . . .

Katarina emerged from sleep and understood that the noise of the train was the hammering of her heart.

This pulled her out of the nightmare and she sat up in a bed, in her brother's house, and tried to calm herself. It was only a dream, she kept telling herself. Only a dream. But it was a memory, not a dream. My journey of shame, she thought.

She wiped the sweat from her face, drank some of the water in the glass on the bedside table and thought about what had happened on the day of the train journey.

It was autumn, and it had got dark early, the last of a long series of Fridays when he had been late home. It got later and later, grew darker outside and now her mother's face had taken on a blank look. 'He won't come. He's gone to her,' she had whispered.

Soon after they heard the shriek of the brakes and the tearing sounds of tyres swerving along the drive.

'Katarina,' her mother said.

Katarina did as she knew she must. With two-year-old Olof in her arms, she left by the kitchen door and ran across to the Berglunds' house. As she pressed their doorbell, she spotted the lorry in the street outside. That meant Kalle Berglund had come home and suddenly she knew what to do. She ran up to the vehicle and screamed up to him, 'You must help us 'cause my papa is hitting my mama and she'll die.'

He climbed down from the cab and ran into his house to fetch his hunting rifle. 'I'll teach that shit!' he shouted.

Karin Berglund was shouting too: 'Kalle, calm down, for God's sake!'

He did not listen to her. Olof started crying.

'You two, come and have some nice hot cocoa,' Karin said.

It didn't make Katarina feel any better, because she had noticed Karin's hands shaking as she poured milk into the saucepan. Olof, however, was given a cinnamon bun and stopped crying.

Then they heard the bang. He had fired his gun! Kalle had shot her father. Delight rose in her. He's dead, he's dead, she thought. She couldn't stop herself laughing.

Olof was crying again, loud and heartbreaking, and Karin was trembling like a leaf in a storm when she ran across to the neighbouring house.

When she came back she had calmed down enough to scold the children. 'Now be quiet, both of you!'

Katarina clenched her jaws to hold back the laughter that was welling up inside her. The little boy swallowed his tears. Karin was on the phone and Katarina realized that she was talking to the police station.

'The police will be here in half an hour or so.' Karin sighed and gave Katarina a hug. 'There, you mustn't worry. Kalle fired at the ceiling. No one was hurt. But Kalle has tied up your father and now he's sitting in an armchair, crying.'

'Mama . . .'

'She'll be all right.'

'I must look after her.'

'No, dear.'

'But, Karin, I've done it lots of times – I've wiped the blood off and I've—'

'Katarina, my dear, the police say that we mustn't go to your house.'

Katarina could see in her face that she was lying.

'If it's anything serious the policeman will call the doctor,' Karin went on. She wanted to set Katarina's mind at rest, but this only made the little girl more frightened. She pulled hard to get away, but Karin held her firmly.

Olof had fallen asleep on the kitchen table. 'You look after your brother,' Karin said.

The little boy's nappy was wet. 'I'll run home and get a clean one.'

'Sweetheart, you'll go nowhere near there. You heard me,' Karin said. Katarina obeyed her, because she saw that Karin was crying.

Then the police turned up, two men in a car.

The images dimmed for the Katarina who was sitting in the guest-room bed in her brother's house. The voices were muffled and vanished, so she could no longer hear what was said.

She did remember that the policemen had been kind, and that she had knelt next to her mother, wiping her face and trying to comfort her, 'There, there . . .'

Then Karin had helped her pack clothes in the big suitcase and the police had phoned her grandfather.

Then the images from the train dream came back to her, every detail clear. She did not want to lose them, so she got out a pad and pencils.

When her drawings were finished, she went downstairs to find Olof and ask him to forgive her, but he was not there. No one was at home.

13

Katarina tidied the kitchen and started hoovering. She wanted everything to look nice when her mother came back. She would arrive tomorrow. It was a comforting thought.

It was such a large house, full of unexpected spaces and corners. Elisabeth had called it 'a rambling mansion' and Erika used to say, with a sigh, that it was hard to keep tidy.

That was true, and it was in great need of redecoration, repairs, new plumbing, all horrendously expensive and unthinkable.

The house dated from the earliest years of the twentieth century and had many period details. Katarina had always admired the characterful architecture with its lovely spacious rooms. But as she hoovered one flight of stairs after another, landing after landing and room after room, the charms of the house faded. This is awful, she muttered to herself. It was built for a time when everyone had servants, plenty of them, and they were cheap to hire.

She had hauled the hoover half-way up the big staircase when Erika and the boys returned. They had been to the indoor market to buy food for the weekend.

'What are you up to now?' Erika said, a little crossly. 'This can't be doing your ear any good.'

Katarina had forgotten about her ear. She thought about it now. Yes, she had a slight headache but, then, she often did when she had been working hard. 'Erika – I forgot I'm not well!'

They smiled at each other.

'You must be sweaty after all you've done,' Erika said. 'Why don't you have a shower and get changed?'

Katarina started to go upstairs then turned to Erika again: 'I just remembered what you said about shame. It's not something you learn, it's an inherent reflex, common among herd animals.'

'Like wolves and elephants,' Jon shouted excitedly.

'That's right,' Katarina said. 'For at least the last hundred thousand years, millions of human beings must have felt shame, based on the realization that survival would be near-impossible if they were excluded from the tribal community.'

'I give in,' Erika said, and lifted both her arms into the air.

Katarina showered and washed her hair. In spite of the dream and her troubling memories, she felt more light-hearted than she had for a long time. She went back to the guest room, set up the spare bed for Elisabeth and made it with fresh sheets. The room was bright: positioned above the large, glassed-in veranda, it got the midday sun.

Still, it was a grey day.

She pulled on black trousers and a red sweater – they were the right colours, she thought. Then she dabbed perfume behind her ears and on her wrists, and smiled at herself in the mirror. She noticed that her face was more angular than it used to be and she seemed to have acquired new lines between her nose and the corners of her mouth. 'I'm getting to look more and more like Mama,' she said aloud, and felt rather pleased.

Erika was putting the groceries into the fridge. She had bought flowers too and left drifts of them in the kitchen sink. 'I thought you might like to arrange them.'

'How nice. Of course I would.'

Katarina divided the blooms between several large and small vases. She started to talk about the house and what hard work it was to look after it.

Erika said that in the beginning she had not complained. 'The satisfied martyr was in control,' she explained. 'Now that I'm trying to get her out of my system, my daily round of tidying makes me want to scream. There I go again, picking up toys and newspapers, books and magazines, half-eaten apples, biscuits and what-have-you from every nook and cranny.' She was getting quite worked up and pointed almost theatrically at the kitchen window: 'Not to mention the thousands of tiny picturesque panes of glass that I don't ever get round to cleaning!'

'On Monday I'll call a window-cleaner,' Katarina said, and before Erika could protest, she went on, 'Another thing I thought about was a dishwasher. You could strain your back cooking and washing-up in your kitchen. Erika, that work surface needs raising and I want to pay for it.'

For once Erika was speechless.

'Well, what do you think?'

'Olof won't let you.'

'He rarely cooks and never washes up, so his opinion doesn't count. Anyway, I'll talk to him.'

'And make him feel he's been letting me down?'

'Why not?' Then Katarina blushed. 'But first I'm going to ask him to forgive me for saying such dreadful things to him this morning.'

'Don't worry, it was just a sibling spat. Besides, he had no business telling you that he had to make whatever it was up to you.'

Katarina wanted to tell her sister-in-law that she loved her, but could not bring herself to say it.

Erika wrinkled her small nose. 'Remember what we talked about yesterday? This morning, there was a collision of two self-images: the strong woman and the good brother.'

'Hey!' Katarina exclaimed.

Erika burst out laughing.

The boys came running in and convinced Katarina that she had to tell them a story. They had decided it was to be about elephants. Katarina went to fetch her pad and pencils, relieved that they did not want to hear the sad end of the story about the girl who walked along the coast looking for her secrets.

Drawing elephants was easy and fun.

She tore off the sheet with the train images and put it on the window-sill. Then she went downstairs to the boys, who were waiting for her in the sitting room.

'Once upon a time there was a little elephant—'

'Two!' the boys shouted.

Katarina laughed. 'OK.'

About an hour later they heard Erika preparing supper in the kitchen. Katarina saw to it that the mother elephant found her two naughty children and led them back to the herd, which wandered off into the distance like a range of rolling hills. Then she went into the kitchen.

'I thought I'd float in politely to see if there was anything I can do?'

'Would you fix the salad?' Erika smiled tightly.

'Are you worried about something?'

'Yes.'

Erika's tone was dismissive and Katarina did not question her further. She put lettuce and sliced tomatoes into a bowl and squeezed a little lemon juice over them. She had discovered that in this house the dressing was served separately.

In the silent kitchen, they could hear the boys quarrelling somewhere in the house about a toy.

Katarina remembered that while she had been telling her story, the phone had rung, insistently and often. She plucked up courage to ask, 'Where's Olof?'

'I think he's in church, discussing the music for Sunday with the organist.'

'I'll go and get him.'

Erika moved as if to stop her but Katarina had already pulled on her coat.

14

The church was only a few blocks away, but Katarina was soon cold. Suddenly the mild autumn had gone and the air was icy. She pulled her hat down over her ears and drew the collar of her coat round her neck.

When she entered the building Krister Johansson, the organist, was playing quietly. She climbed the stairs to the organ but Olof was not there. She had known Krister for some years and they greeted each other warmly. He seemed on the point of asking her something, when the silence of the church was pierced by a child's cry. It stopped abruptly, as Krister played a mighty chord on the organ. But Katarina had grasped what was going on: 'You're hiding refugees . . .'

'Olof is taking them to the convent tonight.'

Krister looked into her eyes. She nodded. 'You know you can trust me.'

They went downstairs together and met Olof in the sacristy.

'I know what you're doing,' Katarina said.

'OK, then you can help us,' Olof said. 'Go back to the house and drive my car here. Park it behind the church. And tell Erika we'll be a quarter of an hour late for supper. Ask her to pack some sandwiches.'

Katarina started to run towards the church door, but Olof held her back. 'Take it easy – no need to break your neck.'

When the car had been delivered, brother and sister walked home together. She put her hand in his pocket and he held it there.

'I came to the church because I wanted to ask you to forgive me for being so horrible to you this morning.'

'I wasn't very nice myself.'

Suddenly Olof stopped and sniffed the air, like a wolf scenting danger, his head thrown back. 'The weather's going to turn bad.'

At about ten o'clock that evening Katarina heard Olof leave the house. She and Erika were sitting quietly in the kitchen. Katarina wished she had a God to whom she could pray. Outside the kitchen window, the sound of the wind through the elms was louder.

'Another storm,' Erika said, 'but we'd better try to sleep.'

Katarina could not sleep. She stared up at the ceiling and reflected on how little anyone knew anyone else – perhaps least of all those closest to them. Elisabeth would arrive tomorrow, her frank, open mother, keeper of a thousand secrets.

Then she must have dozed off, because she did not hear the car return. She woke when someone knocked at her door.

It was Olof. He did not look tired but seemed to be brimming with energy and confidence. Katarina looked at her watch: it was just after one o'clock.

'I'm sorry I woke you, but I have a problem with the refugee family. I couldn't get them all into the car and had to leave two lads behind. Sister Kristina at the convent said that it was all right if they arrived in the morning but I can't take them. My day is packed – I've got a wedding in the morning and a confirmation class in the afternoon.'

'I'll drive them,' Katarina said.

'I thought you'd say that. I'll wake you at about five because you must get them there in the dark – you understand why, don't you?'

Just before five, Erika brought her a large mug of coffee. 'It's so embarrassing not to have a driving licence,' she said.

'You should be ashamed! You have to have one so you can follow the herd. But you're very good at not doing what everybody else does,' Katarina said laughingly.

'The storm's raging out there now.'

'Olof's car is heavy and it holds the road well. I promise I won't be blown into a ditch.'

'Take the winter anorak and boots.'

'Yes, Mama.'

Olof had already brought the teenagers to the church. They were sitting in the back pew, wrapped in blankets. Krister was there too, talking to them haltingly in a strange language. He must have learnt Bosnian – or whatever it was, Katarina thought. Olof produced a detailed map and showed her the roads to take. It did not look difficult.

'The boys have been told to lie on the floor with the blankets over them in case you're stopped by the police,' Olof told her.

'Surely there'll be no police about at this time of the morning,' she said. 'And in this weather.'

'No, that's true – the risk is small. But the smell of snow is in the wind, which is more worrying. Please drive carefully, the car's still got summer tyres.'

'Olof, since when were you able to forecast the weather?'

'Oh, that's not me. It's Erika.'

'Come on, it's only October. And it was practically summer the day before yesterday.' She waved dismissively.

Without turning the engine on, she let the car roll down the slope outside the church, then turned right and stopped for a red light at the roundabout. She smiled at the boys and showed them her watch, then pointed to an hour and a quarter later. They nodded to show they had understood.

The E4 motorway was empty and she drove with the headlamps on full beam. She soon located the slip-road, which led to a winding road through open fields. Squalls of wind hit the car and Katarina gripped the wheel.

After half an hour, one of the boys prodded her back and said, pointing to the radio, 'Misik.'

Katarina switched on the radio and turned it to a programme of old American pop songs that featured several by Elvis. Just what the doctor ordered, she thought, when she heard the boys singing along.

She gave them each one of the chocolate bars that Erika had packed. 'Thank you mitch,' they said.

All was well when Katarina stopped to check their route on the map. They were near the junction with the road that would take them to the convent, where the sisters had become known across the country when they offered sanctuary to immigrants who had been refused asylum in Sweden. A nun was waiting in the doorway. She smiled and held out her hand to Katarina, who recognized her at once from television news reports.

The nun's hand was warm and dry. 'Your brother phoned,' she said. 'A blizzard is on its way through the northern part of Uppland and they're predicting chaotic traffic conditions round Uppsala. He says you should start back as soon as possible.'

'My brother has a hang-up about blizzards,' Katarina said.

'He's not alone,' the nun replied, with a smile. 'The weather forecasters are just as bad. Snow warnings from all of them.'

'Do I have time to have a pee?' Katarina enquired.

The nun laughed and showed her where to go. When Katarina returned, the woman was waiting with a cup of strong coffee.

When she stepped outside, angry snow flurries whirled around her and bit into her cheeks. The gloomy dawn light was growing stronger now, which reassured Katarina as she drove between the flat fields with high winds tugging at the car. Snow whipped against the windscreen, making it hard to see. She put the headlights on full beam, but regretted it at once: it was even harder to see. She dipped them again. Now she was crawling along in third gear with the heater and fan going full blast. She found the switch for the rear windscreen wiper, tried braking and noted with relief that the car did not skid. The snow was filling in furrows in the fields and drifting in the hedgerows but had not yet settled on the road.

This is something else, she thought, relishing the challenge.

Another Elvis song on the radio. Then: 'When you think I've loved you all I can, I'm gonna love you a little bit more . . .'

How silly I am, Katarina thought, and had to hold back tears.

She switched to the regional radio station and listened to the weather report: northern gale, wind-speeds rising to twenty metres per second, heavy snowfalls in northern Uppland. And multiple vehicle pile-ups on the E4.

Oh, God, she thought. The tune was still going round in her head: 'When you think I've loved you all I can, I'm gonna love you a little bit more . . .'

Jack had sung that to her in the mornings. I must get rid of it or I'll end up in the ditch, she thought.

She remembered a song about a French king's marching musicians and sang it aloud: 'We have come from Guyenne and Burgundy, from Brabant and verdant Normandy . . .' The verses were satisfying somehow, with their rhyming couplets and regular metre. She loved order in poetry, as she did classical architecture.

She was on the last verse when a flashing blue light stopped her. She rolled down the window and was told to avoid the E4. Not even police cars and ambulances could get along it now.

'How am I to get back to Uppsala?'

'Let me show you on the map.' The young policeman pointed out a series of minor roads. 'Right at the next turning. Drive slowly.'

Then he climbed into his car and disappeared. Katarina sighed with relief. Clearly he had not heard her heart thumping.

The roads were narrow, with slippery bends and the car

swerved out of control, once at the top of a slope, but each time she straightened it out and it did not seem long before she could see the lights of the city.

As she drove up to Olof's house, her shoulders were aching but she felt very happy. Olof gave her a crushing bear-hug, and the boys tugged her boots off. 'We were so scared for you. But Mama said you'd be all right.'

Erika made her sit on a low stool in the kitchen and massaged her shoulders. Eventually Olof left for his wedding service and the boys went to play with their car-track set up in a basement.

'Elisabeth mustn't drive,' Katarina said suddenly.

'It's all right,' Erika said. 'I've called her and she'll take the train. If it isn't delayed, it should arrive at six.'

Erika's fingers kneaded the tense muscles in Katarina's neck and tears sprang to her eyes as a memory came to her. 'It's so silly of me. I'm sorry. There was this tune on the radio, one that Jack used to sing.'

'Sing it to me.'

Katarina obeyed and soon they were singing together, humming where they had forgotten the words. The tension in her muscles relaxed, her sadness dissipated, and now Katarina found she could laugh.

She had a late breakfast, and stared through the window at the whirling snow. 'I think the wind is dying down,' she said. She turned and looked into Erika's face.

Erika avoided her eyes. 'Katarina, you're going to have a baby.'

It was not a question.

'Yes, I am.' Katarina was so startled she almost shouted it.

'It's a girl,' Erika said.

They sat in silence for a time, listening to the snowstorm beating against the windows. Then they looked into each other's eyes and Erika said, in a low voice, 'I'm so very pleased for you. And for myself and the whole family.'

'I know. But, Erika, you must realize now that I can never cut myself off completely from Jack?'

'It's too soon for you to decide that.'

'I already have.'

15

Katarina was asleep when Elisabeth arrived. She was given a welcoming cup of tea and sat in the kitchen with a little boy on each knee.

'I'm so glad you warned me about the weather and made me take the train. I would have driven because in Gävle it was warm sunshine.'

'Not any more. The storm is on its way north,' Erika said, and looked at the window. The snow was whirling in the air, lit by the light at the back door. 'But it will turn to rain soon,' she added.

'Thank you, O Soothsayer.'

'Don't mock.'

Their warm friendship made them easy with each other. Unlike Katarina and me, Elisabeth thought. Too much between us has been left unsaid. She sighed.

Together Erika and Elisabeth pulled out the flaps of the large dining-room table, covered it with a white damask cloth and laid it with the best china. The boys were talking about elephants. 'Anny, Anny,' they called to their grandmother, 'come and see.'

'I will, as soon as we've finished the table. Then you can tell me the story and show me Katarina's pictures.'

Soon the three were sitting in front of the fire and the boys took turns to tell the story about the two little elephant children who had run away from the herd and got lost in the wild savannah where tigers wanted to eat them and hid in the tall grass and vultures flew high in the sky and might drop down to get them . . .

'Oh, how awful,' Elisabeth said, and shivered.

'Don't worry, their mama's coming soon,' the boys reassured her.

Elisabeth studied the drawing of the herd for a long time. Among the high rolling hills of the adult elephants, the calves were little round foothills. She remarked to Erika that she could see a greater depth in Katarina's drawings now than in the past. Erika nodded. 'Greater tenderness too.'

After a while, Erika said, 'Boys, go and wake Katarina and tell her to come downstairs.'

They soon heard Katarina clatter down the stairs. She ran straight into Elisabeth's arms and they stayed in a tight embrace for almost five minutes.

The boys were embarrassed. 'Why are they doing that, Mama?'

'Because they love each other,' Erika said.

They took their time over supper that evening and enjoyed it. The food was delicious, grilled salmon and creamed spinach. The wine was good and they talked about Katarina's journey through the blizzard.

'You're crazy,' Sam said, 'driving the car in a storm.'

'You're quite right,' Katarina said, and shook her head. 'It was silly of me.'

While Erika put the children to bed, Elisabeth and Katarina washed up. Olof was making coffee. He told them that the nun had telephoned. 'Katarina, I want to tell you what she said about you.'

'What *could* she say? We hardly had time to exchange more than a couple of sentences before I was off.'

'That's as may be – but she said your eyes had the innocence of a child's.'

Katarina blushed.

'She was right,' Elisabeth said.

Erika had joined them, after reading to the boys, and heard this. She agreed. 'Your eyes remind me of Jon's – so direct, with that look of wonder.'

'My development must've stopped at some early stage.'

They all laughed, except Elisabeth, who seemed sad. 'You must excuse me,' she said, 'but I'm tired and really looking forward to bed.'

Erika got up – and froze. 'Ssh,' she said.

In the quiet they could all hear raindrops hammering on the kitchen window.

'That was a blissfully short winter,' Elisabeth said.

'The world will be grey and muddy again tomorrow,' Olof said, sounding almost regretful.

Mother and daughter went to bed at the same time in the guest room. They pulled their duvets up to their chins.

'Are you cold, Mama?'

'A little.'

'There's an electric radiator. I'll switch it on.'

Katarina lit the four candles in the candelabrum too. 'It'll raise the temperature a little and, besides, it looks so cosy,' she said.

'Have you told them about your tiny shoot?'

'No. But it didn't matter because Erika knew anyway.' Katarina told Elisabeth about the exchange in the kitchen.

Elisabeth was not surprised. 'Of course she knew. She probably knew from day one, which was why she poured your soup into that bottle.'

They pondered this for a while until Elisabeth continued, 'Erika is a seer, as they used to call it. She believes she's inherited the ability. Her grandmother, who was very fond of her, was a kind of white witch in their village. It's better for Erika to tell you the story – better for both of you, actually.'

Katarina was speechless with astonishment. Finally she managed, 'Mama, you don't believe in that kind of thing, do you?'

'I believe what I've seen with my own eyes. And that's quite a few things.'

'So, what have you seen?'

But the question was left to hang in the air for Elisabeth had fallen asleep.

Katarina got up and blew out the candles. Back in bed she lay listening to her mother's breathing, which was comforting and made her feel secure. Still, she felt disappointed. She had failed to get closer to her mother – or the other way round.

16

Katarina woke late the next morning when Erika knocked at the door and asked if they would like a cup of coffee in bed.

'That's kind – but, no, we'll join you downstairs,' Elisabeth said.

Katarina swallowed tears: her mother didn't want to be alone with her.

She went into the bathroom, showered and washed her hair, taking her time: Elisabeth would have the chance to go downstairs and chat to the boys.

But when she returned to the bedroom, her mother was sitting in the wicker chair near the window, looking at the drawing in which she had tried to capture her dream about the train journey to her grandfather's home. Elisabeth turned her pale blue eyes on Katarina and asked, 'What's this about?'

'My journey of shame. It came back to me one night recently in a dream.'

Elisabeth said nothing.

'Mama, you can't have forgotten!' Katarina exploded. 'We were in that compartment and the neighbours were walking past the door staring at us.'

Elisabeth kept her eyes on Katarina as she said, 'But we didn't go by train. Kalle Berglund drove us. We were in the back seat of his car. No one saw us.'

'Mama, why won't you remember it like it was? Why rewrite history like this?'

'I feel guilty, Katarina, not only for that night but for all you had to put up with when things went badly. Do you think I could ever forget how you, as a little girl of six, dressed my injuries and put me to bed?'

Katarina shivered with an inner cold and whispered, 'Somehow I never realized.'

'The wall between us was raised by my guilt,' Elisabeth said.

Just then there was a knock at the door and Jon popped his head in. He told them his mother said it was time for breakfast, especially if they had a lot to talk about.

'And we need coffee,' Katarina said. 'We'll come down straight away.'

Erika had freshly baked bread and coffee ready. They were grateful to her for not chatting.

The kitchen was very quiet, apart from the rain lashing against the window.

They went back to the guest room together. Katarina crawled into bed and wrapped herself in the duvet. In spite of the coffee, she was freezing. 'When I woke up after that dream, I could recall the whole day. That terrible Friday,' she said. 'But memories and dreams perhaps arise from the same source.'

'I think so. Memories are coded in words, and language always transforms reality. It helps us pick and choose our past. But it doesn't mean that memories and dreams are untrue, not in the deep sense. Tell me how you remembered that day.'

Katarina told her mother about every detail of that Friday.

Elisabeth's features tightened. 'That seems an accurate account, as far as I know,' she admitted.

Katarina smiled wryly. 'You said that language transforms the past. But words don't come easily to me. My memory works with images and maybe they're more reliable than words.'

Elisabeth smiled too.

'Erika and I have been talking about shame,' Katarina went on, 'like the weird fact that I feel terribly ashamed because Jack hit me. Apparently raped women feel ashamed after they've been violated.'

'What did Erika say?'

'She said that I had reason to feel ashamed – but because I'd been toying with another human being for my own pleasure without asking myself who he was or how he . . . felt.'

Elisabeth thought before she spoke. 'I'm not sure what I was doing. I pitied him . . . your father. I was always there for him, to compensate for his appalling childhood and to make up to him for the constant sense of inferiority that haunted him. I listened to him boast and struggled to satisfy his insatiable need to be seen as a winner. I coped with his jealousy, and I even excused his brutality. I understood his problems – and kept being understanding until I'd practically eliminated myself from our relationship.'

The silence between mother and daughter was heavy with their separate pain.

Still, Elisabeth went on, 'It took years, it was such a long drawn-out process, but finally I lost the ability to stand up for myself. That was when he started to beat me.'

Katarina wanted to cry but found she could not.

'You know, when you had left after your last visit to the forest cottage, I told myself that I must remember. Only then could I begin to understand what had happened. For your sake. So, driving back to Gävle, I decided to write.'

'Write?'

'Yes. A long letter to you.'

'Mother, please. There's no need.'

'I want to do it.'

They decided to go for a walk. The house was empty: Olof had gone to the office and Erika had taken the children to choir practice.

It was still raining.

17

Early on Monday morning, at seven o'clock, the plumber arrived.

'Are you a giant?' Jon whispered.

'That's obvious, isn't it?' the big man replied, and laughed so loudly that the kitchen ceiling almost lifted. He was over two metres tall. He sat down and pulled Jon into his lap. 'I'd like a coffee. Thanks,' he said. 'So, you're a wee Chinese,' his powerful voice roared. 'Now then, you belong to the wisest people in the world, did you know that? And the oldest. Your people invented the compass. And proper writing. You must let your kids learn about Chinese characters,' he said, turning to Erika.

'Of course I will, when the time is right,' she said, smiling her warmest smile and pouring coffee into his mug.

Later, he hauled his equipment into the kitchen and the boys watched, spellbound, as his long steel wire drilled down the plughole in the kitchen sink. After only a few metres, it stopped.

The plumber got up. 'There's no getting away from it,' he said. 'You haven't got a drain. You've got a pipe that ends under the lawn.'

'That's why there's a puddle at the bottom of the garden all the time!' Sam shouted.

'Now, listen to that,' the plumber said. 'The most intelligent people in the world, the Chinese.' He asked if the pastor was home yet.

'My husband will be back soon,' Erika said, 'not that he knows anything about drains.'

'Well, there you are. He must be sorting out pipes going upwards, I suppose. No unholy interest in the underworld. Stands to reason.'

'That's it,' Katarina said.

Erika was laughing, but the plumber was shaking his head. 'Now, our dear Mrs Pastor here, she doesn't realize how serious this is. Your effluent is ending up where it shouldn't. That's illegal. You could be fined, even go to prison, if the worst came to the worst.'

'Nooo,' the boys cried.

The plumber lifted them both up to the ceiling, one on each arm. 'Now then,' he said. 'We'll keep quiet about it. You two and these ladies and I, we'll all keep quiet. And some more coffee would go down well.'

He took the boys outside with him, then called someone on his mobile and negotiated the price of a job. Eventually he came back into the kitchen. 'Is there anybody around who's got a clue about this kind of thing?'

'I do,' Katarina replied. 'I'm staying here. I'm the pastor's sister and an architect. And I've had time to think.'

'Is that so? And what were you thinking?'

Katarina went over to the inside wall of the kitchen, knocked on it and said, 'There's a bathroom just above. I reckon it's linked to the municipal drain in the street.'

'Why should that be?'

'The bathroom was a later addition.'

'Let's go and see.'

So they did, and his drill made a terrific din as it went down the lavatory pipe and disappeared.

'Good drainage here,' the plumber said. 'Why don't you redesign that kitchen?'

Before he left, he held the boys up to the ceiling once more.

Erika was on the verge of tears. 'Surely they can't take you to court for something you didn't know about,' she moaned.

'I believe it's your duty to know,' Katarina said. Her eyes were wandering over the kitchen walls. 'Erika, it's going to be such an improvement. Imagine, you could have the kitchen table in front of the window, in the morning sunshine.'

Elisabeth looked after the boys while Erika went about with a measuring tape and Katarina drew. The kitchen was spacious and it would be easy to fit a counter into one corner.

When Olof arrived and heard the tale of the kitchen drain he had to sit down. 'Oh, no,' he said.

'Oh, yes, and if someone spreads the word, we might be sent to gaol,' Erika said. Then she laughed, and told him the plumber's theory that although the pastor knew about pipes running skywards, he knew nothing about the situation below ground.

Olof did not smile. 'It's going to cost,' he said gloomily.

That afternoon Erika finished taking the measurements, which Katarina noted on her sketches. Then she and Elisabeth took the train to Stockholm.

18

Dread, like a tarantula in her belly, bit into Katarina when she unlocked the front door to her flat. She had planned everything there with such care, decorated and furnished her home so tastefully. Now, the delicate, co-ordinated textiles and streamlined furniture gave her no joy as she walked from room to room, gazing at the colourful paintings, the sculptures, the ceramics.

It had been a reflection of herself.

But she no longer knew . . .

Elisabeth went out to do some shopping.

Katarina sorted through her mail. It included a letter with American stamps.

New York

Katarina, I do not write to beg for your forgiveness. I know what I did is unforgivable. It is also incomprehensible, even though there must be some explanation. All I want to tell you in this letter is that I am desperate, unhappier than words can express.

My wife and I have started divorce proceedings. I have resigned from my job at Berkeley. I'm on my own in New York and my loneliness has helped me to realize that I love you and always did.

We both chose to pretend that all we wanted was a fling, that we were treating ourselves to a fantastic summer. Now I know this was untrue. Or, at least, untrue in my case.

I would be very grateful if you could bring yourself to write to me. Just a few lines to let me know how you are and if your injuries are healing. And if you are still determined to give birth to our child. If you do, then you must allow me to make a financial settlement.

Yours,

Jack

Katarina read and reread this. She was crying, but the spider had stopped gnawing at her.

Later, she remembered what Elisabeth had said about her father. She had pitied him and made allowances for him until she was unable to stand up for herself.

Never, she told herself. Then she wrote an answer to Jack's letter.

Stockholm

Dear Jack,

When I register my unborn child's birth, I shall write: 'Father Unknown'. The little girl I shall have has nothing to do with you. As I have already told you, I will not accept any money from you. I do not want you in my world.

Any future letters from you will be sent back unread. However, I would like just one postcard with a truthful answer to this question: did you beat your wife? Yes or no will be sufficient.

The whore from that fucking socialist country,

Katarina

Some Letters For
My Darling Daughter

Gävle, Monday, 20 November

Katarina, All the talk about 'truth, pure and simple' is mistaken: the truth is never pure and never simple. So, writing these letters to you will take time. If I am to make sense of anything at all, I realize I must start with my childhood.

As you know, my father and his first wife had two sons, who were eight and twelve when their mother died in a car accident. It must have been an appalling shock for her family, who mourned her deeply. That was when Katrin, my father's sister, joined the household. She was an independent, strong-minded woman, a widow and, like me, a teacher. You are named after her, of course.

Katrin brought order back into the house and regular mealtimes with good food. The boys were well brought-up with plenty of loving care, understanding and guidance.

After two years, the unexpected happened. No one seemed able to explain it, least of all my father. He married again and chose 'a lady' as his bride.

She was beautiful but fragile – 'neurasthenic', as it was called at the time. Nowadays she would probably have been diagnosed as neurotic. She was ill-suited to life as a rural pastor's wife with a large, old-fashioned household to run. She could not cope with her stepsons, so they were sent away to live with a maternal uncle in Karlstad. I do not think they ever forgave Father. Katrin disappeared. No one knew if she had been forced to leave or had decided to go in protest, given that she was fond of the boys.

Despite her fragility the beautiful new wife became pregnant. With me, of course. My birth almost killed her, as she often said, and she hadn't the strength to look after me. I have heard different stories about how I survived babyhood. According to one, my father paid a wet-nurse but that seems unlikely in the early 1940s. Another variant is that an elderly maid took pity on me and fed me cow's milk diluted with water. Be that as it may, old Doctor Svanberg – you remember him, don't you? – was alarmed when he came to see the baby, who never grew and never cried.

Apparently he was furious with my father, who felt that he had done his duty by offering up daily prayers for his child. But something stirred him into action, and he went to Säffle and returned with Katrin. She became my true mother. She loved me.

I'm crying now and must stop for a bit.

Katrin had a lovely laugh. She did not laugh often, but when she did the sound rang through the house. Everybody would stop and listen and laugh with her. Every time I heard it, I felt that nothing bad could ever happen. That was what her laugh told me.

Katrin would tell me about things in life that are unpleasant but have to be confronted. All you could do was deal with them as they happened.

Like my mother's distaste: she would look me up and down, and wonder aloud how she had produced such an ugly child.

Of course, that stuck in my mind for ever.

Katrin and I would spend the winter in the big kitchen, and I learnt everything there. Cooking, of course, but so much more besides. Flour came from the grains of cereals that grew in the fields and were ground by the miller. The grocer sold the flour and we brought it home. We talked about the sun, the stars in the sky and their names, and the best way to make a pancake batter.

She read stories to me. When she was busy and I nagged at her, she told me I had to learn to read. She cut out letters from the *Värmland Gazette*. First the vowels, then the consonants. I practised the sounds and soon I could put whole sentences together.

I was only four. Father said I was precocious, but Katrin just smiled and he left the kitchen. You must remember her special smile. Her mouth widened but somehow the corners went down. She had a dry sense of humour, rough and a little bitter at times.

One day I realized that my father was afraid of Katrin.

I remember that he was telling me off once for always being in a hurry. He said I was a restless and stubborn child. Katrin lost her temper, slapped her hand on the kitchen table and said, 'My dear Gustaf, you *would* find it difficult to grasp what it is to be bright and quick, someone of real intelligence, because you're slow and too stupid to hold more than a few thoughts in your head at the same time. Elisabeth is clever and, like other clever people, she gets impatient.'

This exchange took place at the supper table, one of the few times when my mother had felt strong enough to eat with the rest of us.

'Oh dear, how awful,' she said. 'So the child is intelligent as well as ugly. She'll never get married.' She sounded as if she were pronouncing a death sentence.

Katrin's huge laugh rolled through the house.

I could not follow the moves and counter-moves between the adults. But, as I have already said, what you hear as a child stays with you. Some phrases are like slow-growing weeds. Generally they take hold and kill off the cultivated plants.

What about my mother?

She usually withdrew to her large room upstairs and was rarely seen. Even so, she affected the atmosphere of the whole house – somehow, she always made her presence felt. The kitchen was the only place where she could not reach me.

In spite of her frailty she survived for years. You must remember her funeral. By then you were almost grown up. The congregation was large, because all of the villagers turned up. Although they had hardly ever met her, the pastor's wife was a legend among them and they wanted to come and watch. All of her smart relatives were there and the bishop himself conducted the service. Father was curiously calm. My half-brothers had refused to come. Only I shed any tears and I cried for the mother I had never had. I was inconsolable.

When we were clearing out her room, I looked for photographs. There were none. Not a single picture had been taken of her since she arrived at the manse, but an enlarged and hand-tinted wedding photograph was displayed in father's study. How very beautiful she was!

On the day of the funeral I asked, for the first time, 'Who was my mother?' What had happened to her as a child to make her the woman I knew?

As usual I went to Katrin with my questions but she had little to say. 'What I know is mostly gossip. But over the years I've been able to put two and two together,' she said. My mother had 'suffered from nerves' since she was little. She was shy and frightened, and had what I think must have been panic attacks. At the time doctors treated such patients with straitjackets in psychiatric institutions. She, of course, went to a better class of institution. When she came home, she was better for a couple of months. Then the attacks returned, worse this time.

Her family was appalled because she shamed them all. What could be done? Gossip hinted that insanity was probably inherited. So, naturally, they were delighted when a country clergyman had turned up and asked for her hand in marriage. Her father – my grandfather, whom I never met – was amused by the man's rustic manners.

I must stop writing now and try to sleep. I'll carry on tomorrow.

Tuesday, 21 November

You have often asked me to explain how I feel about God. I shall try to tell you.

I have never felt I had any kind of relationship with God, perhaps because I heard too much about Him during my childhood. I think the more likely reason is that I never had a relationship with my father. My mother 'made her presence felt', but he was a void.

I have said this to Olof but he finds it hard to believe. He sees his grandfather as wise and insightful, a warm, caring man, who always wanted to look after others.

That's all very well for Olof. Naturally I've said to him that we must just respect each other's views, but I cracked up the first time when we argued about it. I went upstairs to my room and punched the wall, crying with rage that among all those others my big-hearted father had had no time for me.

So?

You know I'm endlessly inventive when it comes to explaining away people's sins and omissions. So I began to try to 'understand' my father. He had surely fathered me by mistake, with a woman who herself was a catastrophic mistake. All of which was, arguably, his own fault. Still, poor Father – poor, kind, well-intentioned Father.

Olof often says that his grandfather was a good listener, but I never talked to him or confided in him.

To some extent I blame myself for that, but on the other hand I cannot imagine how a child can connect with a void. It is as impossible as talking with God.

I notice that I am painting a dark picture of my childhood. It is not true. I had Katrin at the centre of my life.

I had playmates too. I grew up at a time when people still lived as a community in a village. Then we had a school, a post office, a doctor's surgery with a nurse, and even a dentist, though no one went to see him because he was rough and often drunk. There were quite a few shops – a grocer, bakery, barber's. The sawmill was important. Katrin said it kept the whole place going.

Children were everywhere, playing in the meadows and along the riverbanks. In the beginning, they were suspicious of me because I was the pastor's daughter and a 'lady'. I stood up for myself, though. I climbed trees and rowed, which I was good at. God knows where that came from. I even fought, just like the rest of them did.

The boys accepted me, but the girls ostracized me and I was never allowed to join in their games with dolls. Little girls can be so malicious. The shoemaker's two daughters were the prettiest girls in the village and also the most unkind. They confirmed what my mother had said about how ugly I was. Elina said, in her broad Värmland dialect, that I was 'as ugly as a monster' and all the others laughed. I did not understand her accent, but what she had said sounded disgusting. I told her that she should learn to speak properly.

Everybody called me a tomboy, which sounds innocent enough now but at the time had overtones of something different, alien and threatening. As usual, I told Katrin about my worries and she took them seriously. That evening I heard for the first time about social class. It was a sense of social order, she said, hidden in places where it is hard to spot.

'Now, of course it's true when your father says that in the eyes of God we are all equal. From God's vantage-point, there is no difference between high and low. But it is different for us. You've never seen what it's like at home for Elina, Kajsa, Emil and the others.'

As usual, Katrin did not worry about whether I was old enough to follow what she said and understand it. She started with the French Revolution, whereupon an unexpected, almost incomprehensible world opened up for me.

'I'm who I am, just me, and that's it, isn't it?'

'Nobody is just a "self" like that,' she said. 'You have been formed according to a pattern. Others will judge you by how you think, how you choose words and pronounce them, the clothes you wear, even the way you move and gesticulate. I would go so far as to say the class to which you belong determines your understanding of the world. You're a child of the professional middle class and regarded as someone at the top of the tree – in this country at least.

'The village children you play with are aware of your class, and they envy and hate it. They see you, and people like you, as distant, proud folk who've never had to sweat to earn a living. The shoemaker's daughters are pretty, yes – but they're also low in the pecking order compared with you. They'll do anything to get the better of you. I happen to know their father, who's a left-wing socialist – and, incidentally, a man I respect.' She spoke for a long time about the smouldering class hatred that at any moment might flare up. Anger was growing among the working class and therefore fear among those who belonged to wealthier groupings.

I'm sure I didn't grasp much of what she said but it frightened me anyway. I stopped playing with the other children.

Then I started going to school and that made my isolation worse. I could already read, write, count, say prayers and sing hymns. Our teacher wanted to move me up into the next class. She discussed it with Katrin, who agreed. So there I was, the youngest and smallest in the class, still bored because I was still the best pupil. This did me no good. I often had stomachache.

In spite of that, though, I was happy in bed at home. I could read then, grown-up books. I began with Selma Lagerlöf, then immersed myself in Strindberg.

In the end, Katrin was given permission to teach me at home. I only had to go to school for tests. I was as happy as a lark in spring. But Katrin was talking anxiously to my father about what she called 'the socializing effect of school'.

As usual, he seemed to have no opinion.

As you will have gathered from all this, I was a lonely child.

I went to confirmation classes in the spring just before my fourteenth birthday. I could not understand why, but Katrin decided that I would not join my father's pupils. Instead, I took the bus once a week to Karlstad. These trips were my first solo excursions. I liked the city and enjoyed walking along the wide streets and gazing at the handsome buildings.

I stared at the people too. There were so many of them. I remember standing in the main square one afternoon, struck by how many of us there were, how infinitely many.

The pastor in Karlstad was young and handsome. He was also very convincing and seemed an honest man. Still, I sat at the back of his classes, thinking that he was an expert liar.

That spring I caught meningitis. For a few days I was in a coma and Katrin spent long hours by my bedside. I was not unhappy, though. It seemed then as if I was in an almost holy world, where everything was joyful and nothing evil could happen. My soul was huge and I could explore it.

I'm telling you about this experience because it became profoundly important to me. It was perhaps the most important revelation of my life. My illness taught me that, without training in how to use it, your intellect may cheat or trick you.

Lots of love,

Mama

Wednesday, 22 November

This morning I decided to leave my childhood memories because of what I wrote yesterday about how it was to lose consciousness and find my soul. I gained an insight: there is a wealth of hidden knowledge inside every human being. It is impossible to discuss it in scientific terms. Religion doesn't help either: the churches insist that myths and symbols are treated as historical facts. It seems to me that this is just playing games with reality.

That is how I was reminded of Erika.

You will remember what happened when Olof announced that he had become fond of a girl and this time it was serious. He wanted us all to meet up, you, me, himself and his beloved. I can't remember what made us decide to have dinner at your flat, but anyway, we made an effort, cooked a lovely meal, bought decent wine and argued about what to wear, not too formal, not too casual – well, I'm sure you remember.

She's not one of these people you hug spontaneously, so we just stood about in the hall shaking hands. I admit I was thinking: Good God, it can't be true. Not this insignificant, rather ugly girl. Her small figure looked square and so did her face. She seemed almost mute too. She said maybe five sentences during the whole ghastly evening, and each one was flat and rather meaningless.

We over-compensated, of course, in the way we do, and talked ceaselessly. At one point, I said I believed she was studying Comparative Religion in Uppsala and didn't she think it was a fascinating subject? She said that she found it dull.

We sat at the table for what seemed an interminable time. I did not dare meet Olof's eyes when they said goodbye. I was ashamed. Then you and I quarrelled. I said that the girl must have been ill at ease and pointed out how hard it was to be given the once-over like that. Like a heifer at a cattle-market. But you insisted that she hadn't felt either ill at ease or exposed. It was the other way round – she despised us. I said I wished you were right, because I wanted my son to have a strong-minded, intelligent wife. You laughed then, and told me that a typical mother-in-law might be lurking inside me. 'I can't help asking myself if you'll ever find someone good enough for your son,' you added.

I did not laugh, and that night it was difficult to sleep. Olof was intent on marrying a girl who would be content to trot along behind him, like an obedient dog on a leash.

A month or so later, I was lecturing in Uppsala. The starting point for my talk was the author Emilia Fogelklou and the group surrounding her at Fogelsta Manor. The idea I was trying to develop was that each new generation of women has to start afresh, in one way or another, and build on their own experiences. Actually, I don't remember the arguments very clearly, and it doesn't matter anyway.

What did matter was that afterwards I bumped into Erika. She was standing at the edge of a group of women who wanted to see me and thank me. When she came up to me, I almost didn't recognize her. 'I wanted to tell you that I'm not as stupid as I seem,' she said.

I didn't want her just to walk away then, so I said, 'Please, give me a quarter of an hour to say thank you to the people who arranged the lecture. Then I can get away. If you wait for me in the hotel lobby, we can go to my room.'

We stayed there until four o'clock in the morning. I ordered sandwiches and a bottle of wine from Room Service. She sat on the bed with her legs curled under her and I had the only armchair in the room. She told me the story of her strange childhood in a cottage high in the mountains. Her mother had died in childbirth and Erika was brought up by her grandmother. The old woman's name was Laila, and she was the white witch of the village.

Erika watched me out of the corner of her eye when she said that, almost defensive. Of course, I couldn't hide my surprise, but she could also see that I was curious and genuinely interested. She began by telling me about the foresters who were brought to her grandmother with axe wounds, usually in their legs. 'She was so good at stemming bleeding.' She laughed and that was the first time I saw her as pretty. She had an aura of wonder and expectancy about her, a kind of glow. Then she told of how the consultations multiplied to the point where her grandmother had to buy herself a lorry, a rickety old thing that rattled up and down the hillsides. She had provided it with a makeshift bed for the injured men once she had stopped the haemorrhaging. Then she drove them straight to hospital to have their wounds stitched.

'Did she have a driving licence?'

'Nothing like that. But no one reported her because everyone knew of her work. Besides, I think most people were a little scared of her – she was the local witch, after all. Anyway, I went to the village school but didn't learn anything there. I was already able to read and write . . . so I never became – what's the phrase? – socially adept perhaps.'

At that point I was sitting bolt upright in my chair. I said I wanted more wine.

Erika poured me some and filled her own glass. Then she went on, 'You know, it can be crippling. I become practically mute when I meet people like you – my fellow students, Olof's friends and educated people generally. I think a lot, but . . . Do you remember when you asked me about Comparative Religion? I could have talked for ages! But the academic approach turns the great mysteries of human thought into dust and ashes.'

She fell silent. Then she said, 'When people like you and Katarina discuss something, I cannot rid myself of the feeling that you're lying. Not in the things you say but in your tone – the colour of what you say is wrong and so are your intentions. Do you understand what I mean?'

'I do – well, I think I do. You're probably right, too. But when we talk together, it's a kind of oiling of the wheels – we need to talk to get closer to each other – and to impress each other, earn respect, I admit that.'

'I know. I must learn more about you.'

'Try not to take us too seriously.'

Katarina, it was an amazing evening, as you must realize. And when we parted, Erika said something extraordinary. Standing in the doorway she said, 'By now I hope you have a different view of me. I'm not just trotting along behind Olof like a dog on a leash.' And with that she was off, and I spent a sleepless night asking myself how she could possibly have known what I had been thinking at the end of that painful evening in your flat. When I got back to Gävle and calmed down a little, I wrote to her and asked her.

For some reason or other, I went on to describe my wandering about in the light inside my own soul, when I was in the coma.

Later, Erika and I became good friends. I realize that our friendship made you jealous and I understand that. You can hide nothing from Erika. It's as simple as that.

Now I shall have to say goodnight. It is Thursday tomorrow, my busiest day at work, as you know. I'm lecturing on Friday. We'll meet this weekend and I'm looking forward to seeing that house of yours.

Mama

Wednesday, 29 November

You have often accused me of being secretive, and you're right. I could never have been the open mother you would have liked. But, Katarina, secrets change: at first they are all-important and kept carefully hidden. As time passes by, they wither and shrink, become so insubstantial that one wonders why they were secrets in the first place.

That is the point I have reached now.

Writing these letters to you makes me feel that at last we are talking freely to each other, in spite of everything.

Now, where was I before I digressed and wrote about Erika? Oh, yes, my time at a Karlstad secondary school.

That was when I could be what I had dreamt of for so long: a member of the gang. No longer an outsider, but accepted. It had something to do with social class, of course. The boarding-house Katrin had selected for me was full of girls like me, daughters of 'good' families. Miss Elin was a spinster, like Katrin, and earned her living by letting rooms to girls sent to school in Karlstad. Miss Elin knew the rules of the game. I turned up a week earlier than others and she took me to a hairdresser, and saw that I had a fashionable cut. Then she marched me round the right shops and selected nice clothes for me, all the time telling me how pretty I was. The high point was a Saturday afternoon when we tried lipsticks.

Then she taught me what to say, how to say it, what not to say and what not to ask about. More important still was how to formulate a half-truth.

One subject I learnt not to speak about was sex – oddly, because all the girls, in my lodgings and at school, were becoming women. Instead of sex, we talked incessantly of love. All the whispering, giggling, gossip was about love and so were all the bedroom chats that went on late into the night. Actually, what we talked about was boys: ugly boys, good-looking boys, stupid boys, bright boys. Talk of a handsome new boy made the air glow in our rooms. Jealousy might bring us almost to scratch out the eyes of anyone who was seen hand in hand with a new find.

Yes, I was with them, not apart but always a loner: I hardly uttered a word.

They spoke of their dreams, which were about wedding bells and lovely homes, never sex. Maybe kissing, but no more.

Young women obsessed with love often subsume their intense feelings in anxiety about themselves – their figure, hair, mouth, eyes. They spend hours in front of the mirror and discuss makeup and clothes endlessly.

We had several cases of anorexia although, of course, the condition was not recognized then, and no one worried about those starving children. The rest of us simply admired their slenderness, until the school doctor sent them back to their parents to fatten up. Usually that did no good. Klara, my room-mate, committed suicide.

(Some of these memories are painful.)

The boys were just as obsessed as we were, but instead of love, they talked about sex. When a boy and a girl went to bed together, the consequences of this difference between them were only too predictable.

I did well at school. I was taught by a few truly gifted teachers and my enthusiasm for literature and history grew into a passion. I did a special dissertation on Danish writers, focusing in particular on Karen Blixen and Kaj Munk.

At the time, Kaj Munk was a legend: he had written a play called *Jesus, the Jew* and was killed by the Gestapo.

What else? School drama is worth a mention. We staged *Antigone*, using Sophocles' classic text for a big production. I had a leading role, but which one? Who else was in it? No images appear in my mind. That's odd, isn't it? Then came my final exams and the leaving celebrations. I have no memories of those either. However, I had won a scholarship to train as a secondary school teacher and that autumn, I went to Göteborg. For the first time in my life I lived alone. I liked it very much. You have more time for your soul when you are on your own. The city provided me with the means to disappear, which to me was pure delight.

'Are you from Värmland?'

'Yes – could you hear it?'

'Sure. Which part? Somewhere posh like Bergslagen?'

'Not at all. My father is a pastor in a country village.'

The boy who asked these questions discovered what he wanted to know, my place in the social system, and could now move on to his own father, an engineer in a large Götaverken concern. We examined each other's credentials and approved them.

Girl talk at the teacher-training college was less centred on love and romance: dreams are less easy to keep alive when Mr Right attends the same lectures and turns out to be just as awkward, insecure and sweaty as your brothers and cousins.

I remained a loner, but found friends – well, a few – but never confidants. But I liked where I was and what I was doing. I went to parties and had fun. I was a good dancer, which helped.

None of this mattered, though, compared to the greatest of all my experiences: the sea.

During the first autumn in Göteborg I took the tram to Saltholmen almost every Saturday and even on some weekdays, at daybreak, when I had a late start at college. I would sit in the rattling carriage watching Majorna slip by and the city wake up, alone in the first tram of the day. At dawn, Karl Johan Street would be crowded with hordes of men in overalls, walking towards the ferries that patrolled Hisingen.

On the far shore were the great docks and wharves and the Volvo factory. Göteborg was a working-class city, although you did not see much of that in Vasastaden, where the college and my lodgings were.

But I must say more about the sea. I had grown up by a lake and had always pictured the sea like that when I read about it in books. I had never imagined anything so vast and grand.

There was a turning circle at the tram terminal, then a short walk to the beach where rocks emerged from the water. I would gaze and gaze at it.

That autumn was sunny. A strange light was reflected off the water, a light so translucent that objects barely cast shadows. It fell on the rocks and the people on the beach, making blurred outlines clean and distinct. Sitting there, I let that light enter me and encountered again the mystical experience of my childhood. It brought fresh, confident insights.

Once in Västerås, I lost all of this.

I'll be back with you soon.

Saturday, 2 December

So, I went to Västerås for my first teaching post and met my first group of schoolchildren. The young would give meaning and substance to my life as a teacher.

We had been given a superficial grounding in pedagogic theories but only hints about children's psychological development. In spite of this, learning about such subjects mattered more to me than anything else. It did not take me long to form a daily habit of reading in the town library. I read Freud's book about dreams, and lingered, fascinated, over Jung. My most important discovery was Karen Horney. After all, this was long before people like Winnicott and Alice Miller.

Perhaps I'm over-emphasizing the theoretical side. I was a good classroom teacher. Maybe I had learnt unconsciously how to do it from

Katrin or perhaps I had inherited her talent for it. Pupils in early puberty were the most difficult and most interesting to teach. Hormones simmered in their blood and rebellion in their brains.

I enjoyed myself. A group of young teachers would get together once a week, both to have fun and to discuss work. Looking back, we often talked about what is now known as 'conflict resolution' and 'bullying'. We did not know these expressions.

You know Majken well. I shared a flat with her, one room and kitchen in a new block of flats. We sat opposite each other at a large desk, correcting piles of essays and workbooks. At night, we slept in beds placed on either side of the desk.

When spring came that year, we went to the May Ball. I met Sten there and suddenly understood what all the girls at school had been so excited about. I had all the symptoms: I blushed and my heart hammered. I lost my handbag, my common sense and the power of speech. We danced and danced. God, how we danced that night! He told me I was beautiful and I believed him. He said I was the most gorgeous girl he'd ever met, and I believed that too. I felt sure he was the most handsome man *I* had ever met. He was tall and very fit, had attractive, regular features, dark eyes and curly brown hair.

It was only when Majken dragged me home at dawn that I understood what had happened to me. I had not believed in love, and never thought it would happen to me. Now I had fallen in love. He sent me flowers the next day. The card was full of spelling mistakes. I noticed this, of course, but it only made me feel tender towards him. That Friday, he was waiting for me outside the college. He had a car, which was unusual then. He revved the engine, which made me laugh wildly and we drove off towards Lake Mälaren.

He stopped where the road ended by the lakeside. We wandered about, sharing our delight at the tall birches, their bright green buds reflecting in the lake. The coltsfoot flowers had just opened and looked like tiny suns in the grass.

I told him how I felt about the sea, trying to find the right words to describe my experience on Saltholmen beach. He just laughed at me and called me his little romantic.

I was flattered. I really had lost my wits.

Then we kissed. Not long, hot kisses, gentle, tender ones. It was the first time I had been kissed and it was wonderful.

On the way home, I said maybe we should tell each other about ourselves, where we came from, what we expected from life. He did not answer and I thought he felt awkward about it, so I began. 'I grew up where I was born, in a Värmland manse.'

'I know that,' he replied. 'Your mother was an aristocrat and your father a well-known clergyman.'

'How do you know?'

'I have my sources.'

I should have been suspicious, but he caressed my hair and kissed the back of my neck. Then he began to tell his own story, in short, broken sentences. His father was a labourer, an alcoholic. His mother was a sad, angry woman. They were poor.

'It was awful,' he said. 'I was beaten all the time. But I took the beatings because it kept him off my mother.' His voice grew deeper and warmer. 'I had good head for studying and did well at the standard-grade exams. Enough to qualify for technical college. So now I'm a qualified engineer and working for ASEA.'

He was proud of this, and I was impressed. His story could have been lifted straight out of one of the great proletarian novels.

'Do you have any brothers or sisters?'

'No. I'm an only child.'

'Me too.'

That summer he asked me to marry him. Without hesitating, I said, 'Yes.'

One Sunday morning we drove to Värmland. Coffee was served. My father was polite. My mother seemed stunned and said, 'I can't believe you've found yourself such a handsome man, darling.'

I ignored her, but Sten was pleased.

While all this was going on, I went in search of Katrin. I wanted to be alone with her but I was worried about what she might say.

As usual, she spoke her mind. 'You're about to make a big mistake.'

This made me angry, insanely so, and I said things I bitterly regret.

Now, as I look back, I see that that ended the dialogue that had sustained me throughout my growing up. It was one of the great losses of my life.

Not that Katrin and I stopped talking to each other – well, actually, we did. We kept chatting but now it was about things like the weather and my work, and mostly over the phone. She never asked about my new home and I was too proud to volunteer anything. Or maybe too loyal. I had married a man who was in thrall to his emotions. He was tender, but cruel too. His laughter was as overwhelming as his fury.

In the beginning, I was enchanted by him and accepted rough treatment. I tried to reconstruct his violent mood changes into something called 'charm'.

But after a while I became frightened, then terrified. I stopped arguing and entered gradually into a state of abject submission.

I insisted on only one thing: keeping my job. Sten hated it because he thought it damaged his status. My father talked to me about my wifely duties and my mother shrieked that her family would be scandalized and, besides, I'd be a rotten mother if I kept working. At that point, the row was interrupted by one of Katrin's famous bursts of laughter. 'The old girl's clearly not quite with it any more,' my husband said, but was silenced by the look on my father's face. Sten was sensitive to any hint of criticism, and on the way home in the car, he told me that my relatives despised and sneered at him. 'That's the usual way for the upper class to treat people like me,' he said.

During that journey an emotion gripped me that would trap me in our special hell: I felt sorry for him. I told myself I must learn to understand him. He was unkind for the same reasons as the shoemaker's daughters. But the feelings of guilt inflicted by the working class on the upper class is considered only rarely.

I knew nothing about erotic pleasure and learnt nothing about it in my marriage. Sex meant fear and humiliation to me. My body could not lie. And this hurt him.

In fact, he was furious. He told me I was not a real woman. There was something wrong with me. Remembering Freud, I had to agree with him. Around this time, I remembered my mother's eccentricities, and I worried about inherited madness.

Slowly, I became alienated from myself. Like my mother.

He told me I was ugly, and I believed him. My body was wooden. Who could fuck a plank? That was when he started to hit me. I remember him shouting, 'My old man had the right idea!' He wept afterwards, and it worked – Poor thing, I thought – but I could not comfort him, because I couldn't find the words.

Then, one night, he beat me unconscious. He was drunk and bellowed like a mad bull. We were living in a row of terraced houses so the neighbours heard and came running. Karl laid out Sten and Karin phoned for an ambulance. I knew nothing of all that, for I had escaped into merciful darkness.

I was surprised to wake in a hospital bed. The doctors urged me to report him to the police.

I could not do it.

Karin visited me the next day and she, too, tried to persuade me to talk to the police. First that, then divorce, she advised. 'You know that men who hit their women always do it again, repeatedly. You must get away from him before it's too late.'

I wanted to tell her that it was already too late, because I was pregnant. Again, words failed me.

I was silent when I left hospital. My doctor was annoyed. Sten looked guilt-ridden and unhappy when he collected me. The doctor spoke to him, but I never found out what he said.

At home, he wept and begged forgiveness. It would never happen again, never, he assured me.

I did not believe him.

Still, the atmosphere around us was calmer. We had little to say to each other and a heavy silence filled the house. Karin came and went. 'Just dropping in', as she put it. Sten watched the TV while we women sat at the kitchen table with our coffee and chatted.

One evening, I told her I was going to have a baby. She congratulated me but looked a little sad. Then she said something I would never forget: 'There's nothing in this life to match having a tiny baby growing inside your body. Do you think it's a girl? Do you talk to her? You must, you know. And sing to her, and play all the children's songs you can.'

It sounds so obvious, but for me it was a revelation. Tenderness stirred in me and I seemed to come back to life.

It is not easy to find words to describe this, Katarina. But it was you, just a tiny growing creature, who helped me find myself again. I was no longer submissive.

A few days later, Karin accompanied me to see the obstetrician. He was a big man, good-humoured. To my own surprise, I told him about my marriage and the abuse, and the hospital doctor's warnings.

He listened, then asked me a question: 'Are you in love with your husband?'

My answer was as straight as his question: 'No.'

'Well, then, divorce him as soon as the baby is born. You have a profession to fall back on and should have no problem earning enough to keep the child and yourself.'

My thoughts tumbled about in my mind, new thoughts. I was not trapped for life: freedom was waiting for me, I had options to choose between and I could . . . I had to keep a clear head, must not allow myself to become mute and sink back into inertia and paralysis.

Before I left I agreed to come back with my husband. Next Saturday, at two o'clock. 'That's the best time: he can't come up with any excuses about work then.'

When I got home I lit a fire, settled down in the wicker armchair in front of it and sang to my baby. My voice was weak and I cried all the time, floods of tears, which I collected in my hand and spread over my belly. Later, it came to me as a great surprise that during these months of despair, I had not cried once.

When Sten came back from work, I told him I had something serious to discuss with him. I saw fear on his face: 'You're not going to leave me?'

I fell into the familiar pit – wanting to comfort him – and said, 'We're going to have a baby. I've just been to the doctor and he confirmed it.'

Because his reactions were always so unpredictable, I did not know what he would do next. I had calculated that the worst might happen and planned to slip out quickly by the kitchen door and run to Karin's house. Instead he was delighted, took me in his arms and rocked me gently, as if I was his child. He even wept, and as I looked into his dark eyes, glistening with tears, I saw once more how beautiful they were.

But then I said everything the obstetrician had instructed me to say: 'Nowadays fathers are involved in the pregnancy from the start, and during the delivery, so we both have an appointment to see Dr Robert Borg on Saturday at two o'clock.' I lied fluently and steadily, with a clear conscience.

Sten was proud and happy. 'Let's celebrate!' he said. 'I'll pop out and get us a bottle of champagne.'

'Sten, I mustn't. No alcohol because of . . .' I patted my stomach.

'Just a drop?'

'OK.'

We toasted the baby. As the proverb says: 'Where wine goes in, wit goes out.' Sure enough, I imagined for a few happy moments that life could be like my dreams.

Then Saturday came – another proverb: 'Hard arguments belie soft words.'

My watch tells me that it will soon be midnight. I'm rather tired now.

Goodnight, Katarina, my darling girl.

Mama

Monday, 4 December

I thought Dr Borg's consultation rooms looked more coldly clinical than they had last time. The flowers on the window-sill had disappeared and somewhere in the background a trolley stood with instruments ready to be sterilized.

Also, I felt sure that the doctor himself had changed. The white coat was more extravagantly white and his face bore not the slightest hint of humour. He might even have grown taller since Wednesday.

'Please come in and take a seat.' He turned to Sten. 'Let me explain.

When a doctor takes responsibility for an expectant mother, his primary task is to take a full history. This includes everything from childhood illnesses to later conditions or injuries that might have affected her health.'

I was baffled. He had only asked me if I had had rubella.

He went on, 'When I spoke to your wife, she mentioned that she had received hospital care a few weeks ago. She did not tell me why, referred only to some vague symptoms. Naturally I followed this up and contacted her physician. I have seen the file on your wife: it is clear that she was admitted in an unconscious state having been subjected to severe physical abuse. Furthermore, her body showed old injuries consistent with previous episodes of abuse.'

Now the room was so silent that I could hear a fly buzz at the window. I did not dare look at my husband.

Dr Borg fixed his eyes on him, leant forward and said, 'You are one of those cowardly bastards who beat up women. If this occurs during Elisabeth's pregnancy, I shall charge you with murder. Your child will not survive any more abuse.' He turned to me next. 'Elisabeth, you must consider carefully what you do now. You can still have an abortion because we can prove that your husband batters you. Divorce is another option available to you. The third is to give birth to a child who will grow up in what might be difficult circumstances.'

I was so taken aback by this that at first I did not realize Sten was shaking with sobs. He wept like an abandoned child.

The doctor snorted. 'I'm not impressed. I've seen too many men of your sort. Usually they weep from self-pity.'

The sobbing stopped.

The doctor turned to look at me, and now I saw a glimpse of irony in his eyes. 'Your wife may decide, against all common sense, to continue to live with you,' he said. 'If she does, you must have separate bedrooms. Furthermore, Mr Jonsson, you must not touch her in bed or, of course, hit her. If you are at all concerned about the welfare of your child, you will behave as any decent man would.

'Elisabeth, you will come to see me once a week throughout your pregnancy. Get plenty of rest but also go for long walks in the fresh air.

Above all, look to your own peace of mind. Worrying will harm your baby.'

We arranged the next appointment then said goodbye.

As we left, Sten turned in the doorway and shouted at him that he wasn't the only fucking obstetrician in the country. Dr Borg laughed for the first time during that visit and replied, 'You could try the maternity unit, I suppose. They have full access to Elisabeth's file.'

I had feared Sten's rage and what would happen to me the moment we were inside our own house, so I was unprepared for what he said, 'Your doctor's a tough customer,' and his voice was full of respect.

He moved out of our room that evening, carried his bed into the downstairs guest room and made a den for himself with his ashtrays, his radio and piles of newspapers.

At breakfast the next morning we did not speak, not even to exchange the usual remarks about the weather and the news. But he stopped in the hall and mused, 'I wonder how the doctor defines a "decent man"?'

I did not comment.

That day, my pupils were to write essays in my lessons and while they were scribbling away, I had time to gather my thoughts. Mostly, they seemed incoherent, but I must have made some decisions because when I got home I went to the phone and called Katrin. At last. I was crying and stumbled through what I was trying to tell her. It took me the best part of an hour. She did not say much, except, 'I'll be with you tomorrow morning and stay for a week.'

I thanked her and whispered, 'Drive carefully.'

I felt happy and not afraid, even though I knew there would be trouble ahead. Sten detested Katrin. He saw her as typical of her class, with conventional good manners and contempt for people like himself. He was not entirely wrong. He used to say that I was just like her. Of course, there was something in that too. So, naturally, he detested me.

Darling Katarina, I'll stop for tonight. I'm amazed at how much I can remember and how clear the details are.

Mama

PS. I forgot to tell you something that contributed to Sten's hatred of Katrin. We were living in her house. She had bought it and let it to me at a very reasonable monthly rent that I paid from my salary. This arrangement was humiliating to a man like Sten Jonsson, though at the same time he was proud of his home and often boasted about it.

Tuesday, 5 December

I felt a growing unease when I read through what I wrote in yesterday's letter. I've been too single-minded and unfair in my descriptions of your father. He had other sides and I want you to remember them as you read on.

I did not tell Sten that Katrin was coming to stay, presumably because I did not dare to. She was simply installed in the sitting room when he returned from work. He shrank where he stood when he tried to meet her sharp eyes, but his glance slipped away and finally he sank to the floor, his face buried in his hands. He was ashamed, and it was the first time I had seen him like that. At once my reflexive feeling of pity, the need to soothe him, returned.

'Stop acting the fool and look at me,' Katrin said.

He obeyed. She had authority, just like Dr Borg.

'Why do you hit Elisabeth?'

'She is always right, always knows best. It makes me hate her. I do hate her at times – you know, *hate* her! Her body lies to me, she pretends, she pities me. Why can nobody understand what it's like to be a man who's pitied?'

'Oh, I can understand that,' Katrin replied, slowly and thoughtfully. 'What I cannot grasp is why you think her pity gives you the right to batter her.'

'It's got nothing to do with thinking. I go mad with rage and don't know what I'm doing.'

Katrin looked at him silently for a long while. Her voice held compassion when she finally said, 'Many men nowadays marry women who are their superiors in one way or another, wiser, better-educated, cleverer – the kind of women who are almost always right. But most of these men don't hate and they don't hit out in a rage.'

The large room was silent. Then Sten whispered, 'I don't always hate her. I often long for her. But she's afraid of me, she escapes me, she's forever on the run.'

'Does that surprise you?'

This ended the conversation. I had listened to it without saying anything, dumbstruck. Sten left the house and a few minutes later we heard him start the car and roar off. He did not come back that night. Katrin and I got ourselves something to eat and went to bed early.

The next day, I had a doctor's appointment and Katrin came with me. He said that there was nothing physically wrong with me. 'What concerns me is your passivity, this state you call inertia or mental paralysis. What makes you withdraw, Elisabeth?'

'I think I take after my mother. She's ill in an odd way. She seems to have no will of her own, no sense of self, and no insight into others. I'm becoming more and more like her.'

'Do you mean you're showing signs of inherited mental illness?'

I could only nod.

'I'm no psychiatrist, of course, but I've seen most things. Katrin, would you be good enough to describe Elisabeth's mother and her alleged illness?'

Katrin talked sensibly about a beautiful woman, whose mind was unstable, who had a weekly appointment with a specialist nurse and was looked after by 'the maid'. Her wealthy family paid for her attendants. 'She's harmless. It's like having a shadow moving around the house,' Katrin said.

'Not a shadow!' I shouted. 'She's like a ghost, haunting the rooms, the landings, corridors and stairs. She's everywhere except the kitchen. Oh, Katrin, you must have known how she always frightened me!'

Katrin shook her head. 'I'm ashamed to admit that I didn't.' She sounded upset and paused before she continued, 'I think she was profoundly damaged by a repressive upbringing. Among Freud's patients, such women were relatively common. After all, he based many of his conclusions on observations of hysterical women from the upper classes.' There were tears in her eyes. 'I had no idea that she had such power over you,' she said. 'So often, we just laughed at her and her spite.'

'Is she spiteful?'

'I don't know, but if she is, she's not aware of it. She's like a child, lacking self-control.'

'And who says that her daughter could inherit her state of mind?' Dr Borg asked.

'That's just gossip,' Katrin replied. She thought for a while and went on, 'She's got several nephews and nieces, Elisabeth's cousins. They're all great fun and have broken away from the upper-crust mould. It's irrelevant to them. They're all completely healthy.'

Before we left Dr Borg said that, as a precaution, he would refer me to a psychiatrist. 'Nothing to worry about, just an examination and a few long chats,' he added comfortingly.

Naturally, the prospect of seeing a shrink frightened me. The first time was the worst. She was a woman in late middle-age, strong but very tired. She looked at me with wise eyes, holding her head a little to the side.

I thought of her as the Owl. She made me talk. What I remember best, after all these years, is that she asked me a lot about my father. I have already described the void to you. I often cried during my sessions with her. As time went by, I had glimpses of insight. Slowly, I came to understand more. I was no longer incomprehensible to myself.

And then, one day in May, you arrived. Your birth was the greatest moment in my life, ever. I can find no other words to describe it. I won't go on and on about how adorable you were and how you gave my life substance and meaning. Because *you* were a miracle, you worked a miracle in your father. Sten became your papa, filled with tenderness, patience and love. At three months you had an attack of colic, and he walked with you in his arms all night, singing to you.

He had a beautiful singing voice.

No more tonight.

A big hug

Mama

Thursday, 7 December

This is my last letter.

We had several tolerable years together, the three of us. Working together to care for our child served as a foundation for your father's and my daily life together. There was no more talk of love, but a real, trusting solidarity.

You and I once talked about the great love, do you remember? What it is, if it exists – or if it amounts to wishful thinking?

I had no opinion, as I have not experienced it.

I realize that you are struggling with your feelings for Jack and sense in you a longing that might overwhelm you.

Popular culture pretends to teenagers that love has a happy ending. In great western literature, the theme of great love can be tragic, deadly. Tristan and Isolde, Romeo and Juliet . . .

Perhaps I should be grateful for having escaped it. Perhaps love is always doomed, searing body and soul before it moves towards its tragic end. Then again, it may not for many people still believe that: 'We were meant for each other.'

No. I'm rambling, as you must have noticed.

You once said that you felt as if you had known Jack all your life, from the first time you met. Who did you recognize in him – or what?

I've been pondering on this.

Your father adored you. You were his little princess, the apple of his eye, his most dearly beloved. He taught you to run, ride a bicycle, swim, climb trees. He encouraged you to be brave and daring. 'Never give up!' he told you. 'You can do anything you want to do.'

He turned out to have a fund of fantastic and funny stories, which he told you. Together you would laugh enough to raise the roof.

Everything might have worked out well enough, an ordinary, decent if rather dull marriage, if I had not become pregnant again. Dr Borg had left. He was with the Red Cross, caring for the circumcised women of Sudan. I'm sure they needed him, but I felt betrayed.

Tests at the maternity unit showed that I had an alarmingly high level of protein in my urine. I was given medication, but reacted badly to it. The gynaecologist suggested an abortion but I refused. Katrin wanted you and me to go to stay with her in Värmland. Sten wouldn't allow it. I went on sick leave. Sten insisted I stop working. I obeyed, resigned and cut myself adrift from the last anchor of my self-esteem.

In the end they controlled the protein level and the related problems, but I was told to rest. Oh, God, all that rest. I withdrew relentlessly into darkness and mental paralysis.

The doctor came to see me and diagnosed depression. It was only a word. My home was adrift too, untidy and filthy. Katrin came, cleared up and took you with her to Värmland.

Soon afterwards, Sten began to drink heavily. He would sit in front of the TV in the evening, consuming vodka. Later, he often did not come home at all. I remember thinking emotionlessly that he must have found some other woman, and that it should be a relief for me.

Your birth had meant pain and rejoicing. I spent two days in hell before Olof was born. Even so, he had every baby's gift of evoking tenderness. He pulled me out of my paralysis and my love for him emerged, in spite of the darkness.

Sten was not interested in him, but he seemed almost elated as he drove me and his newborn son to Värmland.

It was spring again and white anemones grew profusely under the trees with their shimmering leafbuds. You were waiting on the manse steps, four years old and lovelier than spring. You flew into my arms and then into your papa's.

I do not think you saw the tears in his eyes.

I felt that my mind healed that summer. Not so that I was returned to my full strength but at last I could think about the future.

I phoned Sten in the office, the only place where I was sure that he would be sober. 'Divorce,' I said.

'Never,' he replied.

Later that evening he called me. His speech was slurred: 'Have your divorce but I want the girl.'

'Never,' I told him.

Katrin spoke to her solicitor. He had been helpful about her inheritance after her husband's death. He admitted not knowing much about divorce law but was certain we would have to go to court. 'It's a custody case,' he said.

That frightened me. At school I had come across many children after contested divorces and knew how unhappy they were when their parents fought over them.

It was a wet summer and we spent a lot of time in the manse kitchen, playing dominoes, writing and telling stories. You often spoke about your father and how much you longed to be with him. You missed him so much you'd die, you said, insisting that you cried for him every night.

That last bit was not true, because we all slept together in the old guest room and the only one who cried at night was the baby.

Katrin felt this was related to ordinary sibling jealousy. Before I appeared with the new baby, you had never spoken about missing your father. In fact, you had said you missed me. But when I finally came, I brought this horrible baby and fussed over him all the time. Katrin was probably right.

When the autumn came, all three of us returned to Västerås. I had given way again.

Weekdays went well. I knew he was seeing another woman and felt sorry for her.

But he formed a new habit: on Friday nights he came home to beat me. The rest you know. You were there and you have an excellent memory.

I'm bored with myself now. I don't think all this writing has taught me anything new. On the contrary, perhaps: some things seem harder than ever to understand.

Tomorrow I shall post all these letters. We'll talk when we meet.

Mama

19

Katarina saw the letters as soon as she unlocked the front door. Three fat A4 envelopes, each one bearing a small fortune in stamps.

Her first thought was: I daren't.

Later on she told herself she was tired. She was working on a large suburban construction project that meant endless meetings, arguments and laughter, clashes of opinion, new ideas and new angles on old problems. There were four architects in her studio, all creative people, just wacky enough to make working together exciting and fun. Katarina kept herself a little apart in this project but thought no one noticed. No one outside the family knew about the shoot inside her.

She made herself a hearty supper. Then she unplugged the telephone and went to bed. She took the letters with her. By midnight she had read them all. She did not look at the clock before she phoned Gävle.

'I'm asleep,' Elisabeth muttered.

'I'll come and see you. I'm driving up tonight.'

'No, you're not! There's an ice warning on all major roads.'

'OK, I'll take the train tomorrow morning.'

'Don't. I'm off for a conference in Malmö. Besides, you're meant to be in Uppsala to look at Erika's kitchen.'

'Oh, I'd forgotten that.' She was disappointed.

'For God's sake, what have you got to tell me that's so important you have to call me in the middle of the night?' Elisabeth asked.

'Just that you're like a hen hypnotized by a chalk line,' Katarina answered. Then she hung up, and fell asleep the moment she had turned off her bedside light.

20

Jack was living among the homeless in the Bronx. Now his world was litter-strewn streets and filthy stairways to decaying buildings. He was popular among the rough sleepers, because he always had money. Or almost always. There were days when he drank himself into oblivion. No bank there.

During his tenth night on the street, he got involved in a big fight. The police came and Jack, beaten and dazed, was among those who were picked up. He passed out.

When he came to, he was in a cell designed for ten men that could hold thirty. It did that night.

A tooth in his upper jaw was broken and had split his lip. It was bleeding and his right hand hurt like the devil. Still, he could see and what he saw, and also remembered, terrified him. He looked at the wire-mesh wall, the heavy gates and the security guard walking up and down with his hand on his pistol. Then he looked at the sleeping men on the floor. The huge Irishman who had beaten him unconscious was close by, asleep with his head on his arm.

Jack was sober enough to notice the stench in the cell. He felt terrible. He had to get to a toilet but dared not move for fear of waking the Irishman.

He was among the first to be interrogated. Name? Address? He managed to recall that he was in a rented flat, and the address.

Telephone number? He remembered that too.

'OK. You're registered as missing.'

'Who registered me?'

'Your father. Guy called Ed O'Hara.'

Jack's laughter surprised him. It was more like a shriek and echoed around the walls of the room.

The policeman did not react. 'You can go now,' he said brusquely. 'You'll be fined.'

Jack got his belt back and his wallet. Then he persuaded a reluctant taxi-driver to take him to the address he had remembered during the interrogation.

He had never stayed under a shower for such a long time, or used so much soap. He found some clean clothes, shoved the old ones into a bag and threw them into the bin. He was shaking like a leaf, hands, legs, oh, God, all over. He knew how easily he could cure it but crawled into bed instead. 'No more,' he said aloud.

When he woke some hours later, the words remained with him in the dull room, as if carved in stone. No more.

He knew what lay ahead. First the horrors of withdrawal, then the craving. And how they would all chase him, mother, sister, guilt. But first he had to confront the worst: Katarina.

He was hungry and took the lift down to the street. He bought some hamburgers and a loaf. Oh, and coffee. He needed coffee. He brewed it strong and ate a hamburger on a slice of bread. His stomach rebelled but calmed down after a cup of coffee. When he had finished eating, he went back to bed and fell asleep.

When he woke again, a new day had begun. Grey light was seeping through the threadbare curtains, illuminating the torn wallpaper on the walls. It revealed the faded pattern. Once, there had been roses.

A new day, another day without hope. He needed a whisky badly. Just one shot, for God's sake.

Then he remembered the police cell, the Irishman, the fear.

When he shaved, the broken tooth wobbled and started to ache, but it did not cause him as much agony as he felt when he saw his face in the mirror. It was swollen and bruised, and his eyes were bloodshot.

He made some more coffee. While he was drinking it, someone pressed the doorbell over and over again, insistently. The police, he thought. His gullet contracted and he almost stopped breathing.

He made himself swallow and took a couple of deep breaths. It has to be about the fine, he told himself, and went to the door.

They stood and looked at each other for what seemed a long time.

Jack's first reaction was strange. How alike we are, how appallingly alike, he thought. Same mouth, same high forehead. His eyes are as coldly grey as mine.

Then he realized that his father was crying.

Jack pulled himself together and said, 'Come in, for Christ's sake. You can always holler at me. Whipping me is not an option – I'm bigger than you.'

There was only one chair in the room. Jack swept the clothes off it. 'Here, sit on the fucking chair. And stop crying.'

'I'll try to.'

The silence in the room expanded into a black emptiness. Jack made an effort. 'Coffee? I've just fixed some.'

'Sure, thanks.'

They drank it. Neither dared speak, but the emptiness around them seemed to lighten a little.

Christ almighty, Jack thought, fearful that he would sense tenderness in the silence. I don't fucking want it. I've hated him for as long as I can remember and it's become part of me. Hating him is all I know. 'Why did you come here?' he asked.

The answer came slowly, his father stumbling over the words. 'I got to hear . . . Evelyn said . . . you'd beat it . . . left your mother. That's . . . what I did . . . once. I know . . . what it's like.'

'You got away after ten years. It took me thirty.' Jack tried to laugh but instead found himself shouting, 'You abandoned two kids! Left them to the attentions of a vampire. Did you ever think about that?'

'Every day of my life.' Now Ed spoke strongly.

It might be true, Jack thought. He suddenly remembered the solicitor, who had called once a month to make sure that the household was running properly and that there was enough money. And then there was the doctor, who visited even more frequently. He always talked to Jack and Evelyn, would even stop by to tell them stories, sitting on a bench in the garden.

'Your father's spies,' his mother had called them. After they had left, she got the headache that made her scream and frightened the children.

Now Jack looked straight into his father's eyes and, for the first time, they truly saw each other. Jack found it hard to ask the question that tormented him. Finally, he said, 'Why did you hit me?'

'Because I was such a fucking idiot! I thought I could beat her out of you. Jack, there's no excuse. I just couldn't bear the sight of her eating you up, right in front of my eyes.' He paused, then found the strength to carry on: 'I was insane. In my mind it wasn't you I was hitting. It was her. And I drank. I was never sober.'

'Did you hit her too?'

'I guess I did.'

They stared into each other's eyes. After several long minutes Jack broke away. He turned abruptly, spilled his coffee into the bed, as he sat down, then grabbed the pillow and pressed it to his face. Sheltered by it, he could recall the scene in Stockholm, image by image, word by word.

' "My mother is ill. Cancer,' he said.

'Have you spoken to her doctor?'

'No . . .'

'Surely you've talked to your wife?'

'She'll just say that Mom's manipulating me." '

He had seen doubt darken Katarina's eyes, and it had awakened a blind rage inside him. Then she had told him she was going to have a baby. That was when he had hit her.

Jack's whole body was shaking now. Awkwardly, Ed came to sit next to him on the bed, and put his arm round his son's shoulders.

It took Jack time to control himself. Then he said, 'I've got a broken tooth. Do you know a good dentist?'

It was like a dream to hear Ed speaking on the telephone: 'My son's been in a fight. You got a chance to see him? Five thirty. Great, thanks.'

21

Afterwards Jack couldn't remember packing his bag, throwing clothes on top of a pile of cassettes, photographs and notes, or Ed hailing a taxi. All he remembered was what was said in the car.

'I've got to tell you: I'm in a relationship with a woman who's refusing to marry me,' Ed told him.

'Why?'

'Ask her. Anyway, I think you'll like her.'

A few hours later, he was shown into the large hall of a magnificent ten-room flat in Manhattan. It was all so elegant that he was almost overwhelmed. He was standing opposite a woman who smiled at him, a startlingly white smile in a black face.

Ed could hardly hide his pride. 'Janet, meet my son, Jack.'

Jamaica, Jack thought at first. It's in the dancing way she moves. But the deep shade of her skin is not quite right for Jamaica. A grandfather from Sierra Leone? The narrow, slightly aquiline nose – could she be part Creole? Her eyes made him lose track. They had the depth of the Indian Ocean.

They shook hands. She seemed friendly but matter-of-fact.

'You remind me of someone,' he said. It was difficult to speak: he had toothache and his face was plastered with gauze-pads.

'I hope it's someone nice,' she replied.

Just that moment, he knew who it was. Janet reminded him of Elisabeth Elg, Katarina's astonishing mother. Both were intelligent and direct, both faces had laughter-lines round eyes and mouth.

'Yes, she is,' he said. 'One of those women you trust instinctively.'

'Great. I hope you'll trust me when I tell you you're welcome to stay over tonight. And to have some of the soup I've got ready for you.'

'Thanks, I'd like that.'

She disappeared into the kitchen.

Jack turned to his father, amazed and, oddly enough, angry. 'Christ, how did you get together with a woman like that?'

'I don't know. But maybe . . . well, as you kind of suggested, Christ our Lord himself . . .'

'Are you getting religion?'

'Maybe. She's a Christian.'

In the large, rustic kitchen, Janet served a thick soup with plenty of meat in it, and bread that tasted freshly baked. They ate in silence. Jack realized that Janet was aware of the atmosphere between his father and himself. Also, that it did not bother her.

An hour or so later he went to bed in one of the guest rooms. He slept deeply, but had dream-like recollections of someone coming in to look at him from time to time during the night.

The next morning his toothache had gone and the face in the mirror looked more human, though still bruised and swollen. He nodded to himself and thought, maybe, after all . . .

The thought frightened him.

The craving for whisky tore at his gut.

They stayed at the breakfast table for a long time. Ed seemed tense but Janet was as relaxed and sunny as a spring morning. Later they went to sit in the light, spacious drawing room with their coffee. Jack looked around the room and said, 'Do you like Scandinavian design?'

'I really do,' Janet told him. 'I love functional simplicity.'

Katarina might have said something like that, Jack thought. Suddenly he felt vulnerable.

Janet saw the pain in his face but did not change the subject: 'You stayed in Sweden for six months, didn't you? Did you like it there?'

I mustn't cry, Jack told himself and clenched the muscles in his face. 'I really did,' he said. 'Fascinating place.'

Ed did not realize that they were in landmined territory. 'I've gathered that the Swedes are obsessed with social justice or equality or something – everyone's got to have a share of everything. The unions are power-mad and the taxes something else. Unbelievable.'

'That's it, more or less,' Jack replied. 'But there's clean water in the lakes and rivers, free health care, no slums and hardly any beggars. They've got a name for their system: the People's Home. They take great pride in it.'

'I call it socialism,' Ed said.

American-style conversation, Jack thought. Here in the States you rarely meet people who take politics seriously. He asked for more coffee.

Following his own line of thought, Ed said he knew a guy who reckoned that all Scandinavians suffered from melancholia of an unusually severe Lutheran variety.

Jack surprised himself by almost losing his temper. 'Tell you what, I'll show you some Swedes who're suffering from it.' He got up, laughing although his face hurt, and asked Janet, 'Do you have a slide-projector?'

'Sure. There's a little cinema too.'

Jack went to fetch his pictures, and when he came back, they moved into the comfortable armchairs in the cinema.

Janet unrolled the white screen and set up the projector. Jack checked through his boxes and suggested that they should start with some views of central Stockholm. He started with the classic one: a shot across the area of Lake Mälaren called Strömmen, with the castle in the background, then a couple of the Old Town. 'Their culture is a few years older than ours, of course,' he said, with a touch of irony.

'You can see this sort of thing in every single European city,' Ed said. 'And Prague's better-looking.'

'OK. But watch out for the next one. You've never seen this before.'

It was a view of a sloping beach in the middle of the capital city. It was swarming with people in swimsuits and naked children, running in and out of the water. The water is clean,' Jack explained. 'Hundreds of thousands of sewers drain into water-treatment plants. Paid for by taxes.'

Ed was speechless.

'Here are some . . . close friends of mine. They're extreme cases of that Lutheran melancholia.'

Elisabeth, a close-up of her face. 'Janet, that's the woman you reminded me of.'

She burst out laughing. 'You're joking!'

'No, I'm not,' he said.

His hands were shaking as he looked for the next slide.

There on the screen was Katarina, smiling broadly.

'Good Lord, she's beautiful!' Ed said.

'There are plenty of lovely girls in the world, but I've rarely seen someone whose personality shines out so strongly,' Janet said.

'The two of us went sailing together in the archipelago not far from the city,' Jack told them.

'Hey, don't take away the picture of the girl,' Janet said.

'I've got more.'

And there she was, walking along the water's edge: naked, beautiful, perfect.

Ed drew a deep breath.

Jack laughed. 'Like I said, a typical case of puritan melancholia! Far too much free healthcare and equal pay and equality between the sexes. Not to mention nursery places for all the kids and an undisputed right to abortion at the state's expense.'

They sat in silence for while until Janet said, I'd like to see more of her.'

He showed them pictures of Katarina holding on to the mast of the yacht, her hair flying in the wind, of Katarina trimming a sail while holding the rudder and laughing into the wind. Her face seemed so alive that they felt they could hear her laughter.

Ed asked about her family.

'Her mother lectures in modern literature. Her brother is a pastor in a cathedral city called Uppsala. She's an architect, well paid, very independent,' Jack told him.

Janet could hear from his tone that he was close to breaking down, but she risked her question: 'Do you love her?'

'Yes, I do.'

'What happened?'

'I beat her up, almost to death.'

He threw the slides on the table and ran out of the room. Then they heard the front door slam behind him.

22

When Katarina woke on Saturday morning, she felt ashamed about the phone call to her mother in the middle of the night. Besides, she thought, I shouldn't have said what I did about the hypnotized hen. I must call her again and say I'm sorry.

No one answered in Gävle. Elisabeth had already boarded the flight to Malmö.

Katarina made breakfast, but did not feel like eating. Before she got ready to see Olof and Erika, she reread her mother's letters. In daylight, they were even more painful.

The old house in Uppsala was full of life. The huge plumber was back, with three smaller copies of himself, his three boys, who all had their father's powerful laugh.

Erika's children were awestruck by them but soon the five were running about wildly in the rooms and corridors of the big house, laughing and shouting. When the plumber got cross and roared at them to calm down and shut up, they crawled behind the sitting-room sofa. For a while, they were as quiet as mice. But it didn't last and the chasing about, up and down stairs and along landings, started again.

When the whole horde poured into the kitchen, the big man waved his arms in the air and called out in desperation, 'Will no one lock up these pygmies in the basement?'

'Let's try the car-track,' Olof said, and disappeared with the children in tow.

A sense of quiet endeavour returned to the kitchen. The work on the floor had just been completed. The old pine planks had been covered by unobtrusive vinyl. Erika had been regretful, but Katarina had insisted: 'It will be easy to keep clean.'

For once the plumber looked grave. He was worried about ventilation in the kitchen. 'We've got a problem,' he said. No one had remembered that the new cooker would need an extraction fan and ducting.

'My fault,' Katarina said. 'The drawings I gave you were rather slapdash.'

'Actually, they were unusually detailed for an architect. It's just that we all forgot about the ventilation issue. We could send the cooking smells into the old bathroom, but you wouldn't want it smelling of fish and bacon and suchlike.'

Erika laughed. 'That's all right. It might even stimulate people's appetites.'

'You can't be serious,' the plumber said sternly.

'Wait! I think the bathroom can be ventilated, too,' Katarina said, and ran upstairs two steps at a time. Sure enough, the bathroom had a sloping ceiling – it was under the roof! Obviously, she said to herself. After all, it had been one of the many late additions to the house.

She hurried downstairs, so relieved that she grabbed the plumber by the arm and dragged him outside into the snow. 'Look,' she said, and pointed. 'That sloping roof is over the bathroom.'

'Well, I'll be damned,' he said. They agreed they hadn't deserved such luck.

That afternoon Erika dished up sausages and bread, beer and milk. Then the plumber and his boys left and the kitchen was peaceful again. Sam and Jon were sent off to watch TV and the grown-ups tidied as best they could.

Katarina was enthusiastic: 'Soon we'll get professional cleaners in. And a window-cleaner. Oh, Erika, can't you see how fantastic it's going to be with the kitchen table in front of the window and a really functional work surface? And a dishwasher! No dirty dishes piling up in the sink again.'

'And new net curtains,' Erika said longingly.

Olof had some difficulty in voicing the question he had been pondering for so long: 'Katarina, how can you afford all this?'

'Well, you might not approve so I'm not sure I want to tell you,' Katarina said.

The children had joined them in the kitchen, and Jon asked, 'Did you rob a bank?' His voice trembled with excitement.

'Of course not!' Katarina told him. Then she turned back to Olof. 'Remember the money Mama gave us, which she had inherited from Katrin? I suppose you saved yours?'

'Of course I did, to have a stand-by. Just in case.'

'Great. It was different for me, since I haven't got any children . . . yet,' she said, and her hand went to her stomach. 'I decided to speculate in the stock market. One of my colleagues knows about stocks and shares, and he helped me. So much so, that my money has doubled over a few years.'

Erika laughed so hard she had to sit down. Olof's face changed first to surprise and then to delight. 'What an amazing sister!'

Sam and Jon, who had not understood, asked Olof eagerly, 'Papa, what did she do? What did she do?'

Katarina and Erika left Olof to try to explain. They were still laughing when they settled down in the sitting room.

'It's all wonderful, but I can't help thinking that the best thing about the whole refurbishment is the plumber and his little boys,' Erika said. 'Remember when he turned up the first time? Swinging our boys to the ceiling and telling them that the Chinese are the cleverest people in the world? And then he must have realized that they're lonely here and brought his own to play with them. It's the first time they've had friends in the house. You know how hard we've tried, dragging them along to after-school groups, but they've been . . . well, it's hard to find the right word . . . excluded.'

'And bullied, I know,' Katarina said.

'His wife is called Ulla and she's almost as overwhelming as he is. She's a primary-school teacher and dreams of setting up a small playgroup for children of all nationalities. Lars is not well off, but he's promised to invest what he can in it.'

After a moment Katarina remembered that Lars was the plumber.

'So, we're dreaming with them. Olof is willing to invest

Katrin's money.' Erika seemed a little embarrassed. 'We keep saying how nice the basement would be if it was redecorated. There are fair-sized windows all along the back wall.'

'It sounds almost too good to be true,' Katarina said.

'There's such a lot of red tape, though. But it might work. Ulla has her teaching qualifications and Olof a certain status because he is a clergyman. Anyway. Hang on, I'll make us some coffee.'

When Erika returned with two steaming mugs and a plate of biscuits, she said, 'It's written all over you that something's happened recently – I think.'

'Mother wrote to me, several letters, in which she told me about her childhood and her marriage. Erika, it's so . . . I don't know. Touching. I've read and reread these letters and now I believe I understand her better.'

They were interrupted by the boys who chorused, 'Secrets!'

Olof had gone to his study to work on his sermon for the following day. His chosen theme was the parable about the camel and the eye of a needle.

When he joined them again, he said to Katarina, 'There's an email for you. From someone in Malmö. I haven't read it.'

He sounded worried. Katarina explained that it was probably from their mother. 'She's at a conference.'

She read it.

'It's a poem by T. S. Eliot,' she said. 'Listen.

> "Where is the Life we have lost in Living?
> Where is the Wisdom we have lost in Knowledge?
> Where is the Knowledge we have lost in Information?" '

'Do you understand what she's telling you?' he asked.

'I think so. Especially with the last two lines.'

She was very still, a distant expression on her face. Then she said, 'I've never had any wisdom to lose.'

Olof laughed at her, Erika shook her head, and both the boys wanted to know, 'What have you lost?'

'I don't know, that's the worst thing,' Katarina replied. Then she smiled and said, 'Come on, let's go out for a slap-up meal!'

Which was exactly what they did.

It was not until late that night that Katarina and Erika had a moment to themselves.

'Did the letters tell you a lot you didn't know?'

'Yes, most of it was new to me. For instance, that my mother was an unwanted baby, almost fatally neglected until Katrin arrived on the scene. I think it might explain her inability to act when we were children and our father abused her.'

'Didn't she ever tell you . . . ?'

'No. Did you know?'

'Well, I did but only in a general way. She told me after I'd been talking about how my grandmother had had to take responsibility for me when my mother died.'

'Of course, I see.' Katarina was hurt.

'Erika, do you know what I think is the most awful thing about it all? Mama still doesn't get it. She can't see the pattern.'

Erika was stunned and had to search for the right words. 'Katarina, you must be mistaken. Elisabeth had two years of psychoanalysis in Göteborg. She unravelled her strange childhood then.'

Katarina was irritated now. 'She was lying if she told you that. I know. We were together all the time then, just the two of us. It was the best time of my life.'

Erika tried to put her arm round Katarina's shoulders, but was pushed away. 'Elisabeth never lies, you must know that. And you went to school every day, of course,' she said.

They sat together in silence. Katarina was shivering with cold and Erika went to fetch a blanket.

'I know there are psychological models for what we do. We can work out connections, distinguish patterns,' Erika said, as she draped the blanket round Katarina. 'It helps a lot, I'm not denying that.' She paused and then she put her arm round Katarina. 'But when all is said and done, most things are still not understood. Life is so paradoxical. What happens to each and every one of us is unique and so is the way we respond. To grief and death, as well as to joy and love. No knowledge in the world can cure your loneliness and save you from your fears.'

'That's what she wanted to tell me with that poem of Eliot's,' Katarina whispered.

They said goodnight, but half-way up the stairs Katarina turned to her sister-in-law. 'Once I asked Mama about you and where you came from. What had made you almost unbearably wise and . . . intuitive. She said you'd tell me yourself one day.'

Erika looked thoughtful. 'Maybe I should follow her example and write a letter. It's a long story, you know.'

'I don't want any more letters. All I do is misinterpret what's written in them. I want to look into your eyes as you speak. And ask you questions when I don't understand. Can't you spare a day?'

'What about the day after Christmas?'

'Oh God, Christmas! It's never come at a more awkward time. Mama and I are supposed to be moving house.'

23

The sun woke Katarina. Its brilliance fitted with her mood: she was happy and looking forward to the afternoon. She had taken time off work and in a few hours she would set out to collect Elisabeth from Arlanda airport. They would drive straight on to the new house.

I know she'll like it, Katarina thought. She put her hands over her belly and sang a little song for the baby inside it.

There was a knock at the door. Olof popped his head in. 'It's twenty-two below. Put on all your woollies and join us for breakfast in front of the fire.'

'Coming.'

The house was chilly and Erika was doling out thick Icelandic sweaters. Katarina worried about her car starting, but Olof promised to get it going and even to drive it until it warmed up. She ate three cheese sandwiches, drank plenty of coffee and told the boys she would not be around today to tell them a story. They tried to persuade her, little heads to one side. 'It won't work,' Katarina said. 'You don't want Anny to stand about alone in the freezing airport, do you?'

The car was warm as she drove on to the E4 motorway. What a good little car, she thought, and looked out over the landscape, so soft and beautiful – all brilliant white and long blue shadows.

She arrived at the airport in time to have another cup of coffee. Not right for the little one, though, she thought, and patted her stomach. She promised herself that soon, very soon, she'd go easy on the caffeine.

The flight from Malmö arrived. Elisabeth was among the last off the plane. They smiled at one other.

'Did you get my poem?' she asked.

'Yes, I did.'

'Isn't it good?'

'Very.'

On the escalator, Katarina said, 'I'm sorry about the hypnotized hen.'

'You were upset.'

'Why didn't you tell me you saw a psychoanalyst in Göteborg?'

They were waiting at the luggage carousel.

'How do you tell a seven-year-old that her mother has to see someone who looks after mad people? Every day. And especially when the child is vulnerable, has already experienced . . . and seen . . . too much.'

They were silent in the lift to the car park. In the car, Elisabeth took up where they had left off. 'Of course, I could have told you later, but I didn't and my silence widened the barrier between us. This summer was the first time that I realized how you were trying to fill the vacuum with fantasies about the past – and your own grim memories, of course.

'Do you remember your last visit to my cottage, when we were both washing in the old laundry? That was when I saw all the questions in your eyes. We were standing in front of the mirror, looking at each other as well as ourselves. You'd wondered for so long – How could you, Mama? Why did you put up with it? And that was when I decided to write to you.'

Elisabeth was quiet while they fastened their seatbelts and Katarina reversed the car. Then she said, 'It was silly of me, I know, but I wanted to make it up to you. To give you a happy, secure mother.'

'You succeeded,' Katarina said and blew her nose. When they were through the toll-gate, she went on, 'Anyway, I've decided we're going to have a fun day together, you and I.'

'Good!' Elisabeth said, and laughed.

'Like a hen night, but a whole day of it!'

'Have you got a hen fixation?'

Katarina laughed so much that she almost lost control of the car.

They left the motorway and drove past an ancient church and then a lake.

'This is very pretty,' Elisabeth said.

'Wait and see.' Katarina's eyes were glittering like the snow in the sunshine. 'Just wait.'

'Now I think of it, you've told me very little about the house and the area it's in.'

'It was meant to be a surprise.'

And it was just that. 'But, Katarina, this is no ordinary suburban terrace! It's like a villa!'

'Well, it's called a "chain-house" – meaning, the houses are linked by their garages.'

Katarina produced the keys and they stepped into the large hall. The house was warm and the walls had had a fresh coat of white paint. To their left was a well-equipped kitchen, and to their right, a spacious sitting room with a fireplace and large windows looking out over open countryside.

'Follow me, Mother dear. Now, for the best part of all.' Katarina led Elisabeth upstairs.

The upper floor had sloping ceilings but the large room was lit by a row of dormer windows. At once Elisabeth went over to a window and stayed there, looking out over the meadows and clusters of broad-leaved trees with lake-ice glinting further away. 'That's a lake, isn't it?'

'Yes, it is. It's still frozen but soon you'll look out over open water. The Hanssons, who used to live here, tell me that in spring they would hear the ice cracking.'

The first floor had the same simple layout: bedroom to the right, kitchen to the left. The latter was freshly painted, but the small bathroom looked worn.

'The Hanssons' teenage children lived up here. We'll have to do something about it when we know for sure if . . . well, if we feel happy about—'

'I know already that I'll be happy here,' Elisabeth said. She was close to tears of joy but pulled herself together. 'Where's your bedroom?'

'It's a nice big room behind the downstairs kitchen. Come and see!'

In the end, Elisabeth felt tired and wanted to sit down. Since there was not even a stool in the house, they sat on the sink-surround while Katarina described the area. 'There are lots of young families and lots of children in these new houses. There's a nursery school half-way down the road towards the town centre. The town has all the usual amenities, like a health centre, mother-and-baby clinic, school, library and so on. Shopping too, of course.' She added cheerfully, 'It couldn't be more convenient! Well, except that we'll be rather dependent on our cars. There's a regular train service into central Stockholm, though.'

Suddenly the doorbell rang. They looked at each other in faint alarm. 'Come on, it's probably a neighbour coming round to welcome us,' Katarina said.

She was right. A man stood outside the door, tall and fat as a barrel. His square, bearded face looked as if it had been hewn from wood by an apprentice carver. It was scattered with specks of paint and the odour of sweat hung around him mingled with turpentine.

'Karlsson's the name. Just thought I'd come and say hello. Besides, I fancied you wouldn't mind a cup of coffee, and a couple of chairs to sit on.'

'Especially if you've got an armchair,' Elisabeth said.

Katarina thanked him. 'This is so kind of you.'

'I'll go ahead, then, and start the coffee.'

They pulled on their boots and winter coats. Katarina was thinking so hard that her forehead wrinkled. 'Mama, I recognize him from somewhere.'

'Where, do you think? Who is he?'

'I don't know.'

Then, the moment she crossed the threshold into Karlssons' house, it came to her. The wall facing them glowed with the rich colours of a wild, tropical garden.

'I fancied some warmth in here,' Karlsson said.

'So you did, Viktor Emmanuel Karlsson! Mama, this man, who's trying to look ordinary, is one of Sweden's finest painters.'

'Greetings,' Elisabeth said. 'And can the great master brew coffee too?'

'Certainly can. Let's move on to the kitchen.'

'I'd better not have any coffee. I'm going to have a baby and too much doesn't agree with it.'

'Fantastic!' he said, and hugged her.

'Do you mind if I look around while you two have your coffee?' Katarina asked.

'Be my guest. I live upstairs, so there isn't much to check out down here.' She nodded. It was easy to see why he would use the sitting room as his studio. There were so many paintings stacked along the walls that she did not know where to start. One at a time, she told herself.

Then her eyes fell on the huge triptych on the short wall opposite her.

24

She found the nearest chair and pulled it in front of the painting. Somewhere she heard Elisabeth and the artist rattling coffee cups, joking and laughing.

A little later, he brought her a glass of milk and an apple. He broke her contemplative mood – she didn't want him there and would have liked to push him out of the room. Instead she said, 'Tell me about this, please.'

'It started with me falling in love with the triptychs by the masters of Renaissance painting. The first panel shows a not uncommon theme: Annunciation, expectation illuminated by a kind of blue light – the light of longing. Reverence towards the miracle. Fear too, of course. I put Life itself in the centre panel, I wanted it all to be there: the greatness, the joy and the grief. And then, in the last one, Ageing, Death, and the return to the mystery beyond.'

He fell silent, obviously embarrassed, and scratched his head.

'Please go on,' Katarina begged.

'The old masters saw everything in such concrete terms. Maybe their images of the world were naïve – too literal, or something?' He scratched his head again. 'Maybe they saw further than we do, in some ways. But they painted like children, which was fine . . . then. Just like some preachers do nowadays, the painters understood their myths literally. Trouble is, when you do that, the myths lose some of their potency. Do you see what I mean?'

'Yes, I think so.'

'My notion was somehow to recharge them with magic. Undress the myths, down to their essentials, lose the historical baggage . . .'

Katarina saw that Elisabeth had come in, coffee cup in hand, and stopped a step behind the painter. 'Do you like it, Mama?'

'I'm gripped by it.'

'I'd like to stay here and look at it for a little longer,' Katarina said, and only then did the other two realize how deeply moved by it she was.

They left her alone and her mind sank back into the first image. It was so right, just how she felt now. An infinite spectrum of blues, all the shades of the sky. Fear was in cold white moonlight cast over small soft creatures, but the whole painting was suffused by the golden glow of dawn. The light of waiting, she thought.

She ate her apple.

Then she joined the others in the kitchen. 'I hope you'll let me come back some time.'

'Katarina, you're so pale. We must go home and get some sleep.'

'You're right. Would you drive?'

Before Katarina fell asleep that night, she mused on how amazing it was that the light at the centre of life was turquoise and that it fell on tiny orange-coloured shoots.

25

The following morning they woke early.

'I should be feeling all solemn and nostalgic – the last day in the old home, that kind of thing,' Katarina said.

'And do you?'

'Not really. Just looking forward to moving into the house.'

They started packing china and books. A few hours later, Erika and Olof turned up to give them a hand, having left the boys with Ulla, the plumber's wife.

Then the Hanssons arrived with the removal lorry, piled high with their furniture.

'We'll be on our way early tomorrow morning,' Katarina said. 'The cleaners are booked for ten o'clock, so the flat will be tidy for you when you move in.'

'It's going to be great,' Kerstin Hansson said, and Katarina nodded. She felt slightly peeved at the thought of the Hanssons' things filling her flat: the fine antique furniture, handsome leather sofas set out on thick square carpets, and the rich folds of heavy curtains at the windows.

It was chaotic, of course, emptying their own removal lorry when it had stopped outside the house by the lake. The chaos took only a few hours to clear, though, because Katarina had planned beforehand where every piece of furniture would go. Soon enough, she could concentrate on hanging new net curtains in all the windows.

The telephone engineer called. Just after the telephone had been connected, the electrician arrived and fitted the computer, the TV and the hifi. He provided some useful extension flexes and approved of Katarina's light-fittings: 'Cool.' Then he put everything into place, plugged it in and left.

The next visitor was a woman, sharp-faced and a little sad. She introduced herself: 'My name is Kristiansson. I live next door and thought I should bring you the traditional pot of moving-in porridge.'

'How nice!' Elisabeth said. 'And how very kind.'

'I'll fix some coffee for us all,' Katarina said.

Then Viktor Emmanuel showed up. He had brought 'the traditional moving-in bottle of aquavit', as he put it.

'You ladies are well organized,' he remarked, as he watched Elisabeth at the fridge, taking out the sandwiches they had bought.

'Not me,' Elisabeth said. 'But my daughter's remarkably good at planning ahead.'

The house was almost in order by the time they settled in the kitchen for a sandwich lunch. Mrs Kristiansson was flushed with pleasure at the praise for her 'porridge', which was actually rice pudding. When she left, she mentioned that she had seven pot-plants and they were welcome to take cuttings at any time.

The next day they boarded the airport bus. It was time to deal with Elisabeth's things in Gävle. They argued about her much-loved old bed. 'No way are we taking it with us,' Katarina said. 'It's over twenty years old.'

'There's nothing wrong with it!'

'Oh, no? Its base is worn-out and sagging, the mattress is lumpy and the headboard's dirty. Haven't you heard of dust mites?'

'I need my bed!'

'You don't because they're delivering a new one today, just like this. It's a present to you from me.'

'You're mad! Can't you spend your money on something sensible?'

'It *is* sensible. I've got a mother with a dodgy back. It couldn't have been better spent.'

The removal lorry left Gävle on Thursday morning. Elisabeth travelled in the lorry and slept almost all the way. Katarina drove her mother's old car to Stockholm. She felt Elisabeth ought to drive something better and newer, but the money was running out.

They started nest-building. It took them only a couple of weeks to get everything as they wanted it.

'Order,' Elisabeth said. 'I've dreamt of it all my life.'

They were pleased with themselves and each other when they locked up their house and left to celebrate Christmas in Uppsala.

26

After Jack had left, the large Manhattan flat seemed almost unbearably silent. It was as if time had stopped.

Neither Ed nor Janet could find any words with which to break the silence. They would look back on that Saturday as one of the longest days in their lives.

The minute hand on the clock crawled round, as if it was measuring the hours.

The phone rang, messages were recorded.

Then came the moment when Janet's huge eyes focused on Ed and she said, 'It can't be true.'

'It must be. I asked him yesterday if he planned to return to that Swedish university and he said he couldn't. The reason is that the Swedish police have him on their wanted list.'

'So it's true, what he said he did to that girl?'

'I suppose so.'

'Ed, it's beyond belief. And unforgivable.'

'I know. From my own . . . experience. As you know. Anyway, from the number of abused women you see in the course of your work, well . . . you know it happens.' He groaned.

For a while, they said no more.

Later they had a simple kitchen supper and drank a couple of beers. Then Janet's brain was working again.

'I'm the professional here,' she said. She gave Ed a sleeping-pill and told him to go to bed. She stayed by the telephone and made a number of calls. It did not take her long to locate Pastor Olof Elg in Uppsala, Sweden.

'You'd better not call right now,' the operator said. 'It's the middle of the night in Sweden.'

Who fucking cares? Janet thought, and rang the number. Eventually a sleepy voice answered, in a language she did not understand. 'Do you speak English?'

'I do.'

She told the man at the other end of the line that she was a lawyer and that she had . . . well, a contractual obligation to a man who believed that he was wanted for the murder, or possibly manslaughter, of a Swedish woman. 'He's desperate, close to suicide,' she said, and immediately felt ashamed.

'For God's sake,' the Swedish voice said.

'Yes, that's right, for God's sake,' Janet said. 'You're a member of the clergy, and I'm a Christian.'

'You can tell Jack O'Hara that Katarina has recovered fully and is looking forward to the arrival of the baby.'

'Baby?' Janet could hardly believe her ears.

The voice from the other side of the Atlantic spoke again: 'How do I get hold of Jack?'

'Actually, he's gone missing but I have every hope . . . that he . . . well, that the police have picked him up by now. They will contact his father. There's a missing-persons' report circulating about him. May I call you back?'

'Please do, as soon as you can.'

Janet hurried into Ed's room. He was asleep. No point in waking him, not yet anyway.

She went off to do some chores, the supper washing-up, putting Jack's slides in order, tidying. It did not help. Her heart still beat too fast and her mouth felt dry.

In the end she went to her secret cupboard and poured herself a large glass of whisky.

She drank it and then the telephone rang. A woman with a deep voice said, 'My name is Erika Elg. I'm married to Olof. He's in church now and I promised him I'd phone. Do you have any news of Jack?'

'No, I don't.' Janet's voice cracked. She felt ashamed that she could not be businesslike. 'I'll let you know as soon as we find him. Thanks for calling, Erika.'

Ed had woken up when the phone rang. 'Who was that?'

'Oh, relax. I phoned that girl's brother. In the middle of the night. Listen to this, I recorded the call.'

She started the tape and increased the volume when the voice said, 'You can tell Jack O'Hara that Katarina has recovered fully and is looking forward to the arrival of the baby . . .'

Ed caught his breath. She sat next to him. 'I'll call the police,' he said. 'Jack must hear this.'

'Ed, leave it,' she said. 'Trust him.'

They stayed sitting close together on the sofa. Then they heard the door open and he was standing in front of them.

'Why are you sitting here in the dark?' He turned on some lamps. 'I behaved badly,' he said. 'I'm sorry. But, Dad, listen, I made it! I've been walking the streets in this fucking city, counting the bars. Any idea how many drinking holes there are? Hundreds. I'm not kidding. But I didn't go into a single one. Not one drink, all evening.' He threw back his head and laughed, not from happiness but from a sense of victory. 'I'm hungry,' he said. 'Janet, is there any of that soup left?'

Janet laughed. 'Maybe. But first there are more important things to do.'

She told him how she had got hold of the number to Pastor Elg. 'It was night-time over there, but I didn't worry about that.' She switched on the tape. 'Listen to this.'

Jack turned so pale that Janet was worried. 'Jack,' she said, in her most authoritative voice, 'don't faint. Pull yourself together. Pastor Elg is sitting by his phone, waiting for a call from you.'

Jack's hands were shaking so badly that she had to help him with the dialling. Then she and Ed left him alone and he had to confront the English-sounding voice that had given him hell in the Stockholm flat. This time, the voice asked forgiveness for what had been said in the past. 'You must realize that I was desperate – and furious after a night waiting around at the hospital. It took them all night to do the operation. I was insane with rage for days afterwards, so I said some harsh things when you phoned.'

'What you said was true. I deserved every word.'

'What you deserve and don't deserve is between you and God. No man should judge another as I did then.'

There was a long silence. Jack couldn't speak.

'Listen,' Olof went on, 'Katarina is fine. What I said about the police never happened. She refused to bring a charge against you.'

'She refused?'

'That's right.'

'How am I to interpret that?'

'You must realize one important thing: I cannot go behind my sister's back and negotiate with you on her behalf. And, in her view, the baby is her responsibility and hers only.'

'That's true.'

'You might think so, but Elisabeth does not agree. She argues that no mother has the right to stop a child seeing his or her father,' Olof said. After another long silence, he continued, 'I can't promise anything with regard to Katarina, of course. I don't know what she thinks or feels about you. But I will urge her to send you an invitation to the child's christening. Then it's up to you. Does that sound fair?'

'Fine.'

Jack slept for the rest of that long Saturday, enveloped in merciful darkness. He woke in grey twilight, watched the rain wash over the huge city, and told himself he must have been dreaming.

He walked on shaking legs along the corridor to Janet's room. She was asleep. She's just as beautiful asleep as awake, he thought. 'Janet,' he whispered 'I've got to know this. Did that call really happen?'

She woke immediately. 'Of course,' she said crossly. 'I recorded it so you can listen to it any time. And don't you dare come and wake me again without bringing me a big cup of coffee.'

Erika's Story

'I was illegitimate. My mother died when I was born. Nobody said so openly, but I believe most people, who knew the circumstances, drew sighs of relief.'

It was the day after Christmas, and Erika and Katarina were talking together, just as they had hoped to. Elisabeth, Olof and the boys were safely out of the house at the cinema.

Katarina was lighting the fire but what Erika said upset her so much that she almost dropped the match. 'Surely no one can feel relieved at the death of a young mother!'

'You must be right. It was a hard thing to say. Besides, her death did not remove the shame because I was still there, crying my head off. The whole village could hear, or so they said.'

'Erika, you were born in the early seventies. The old stigma of illegitimacy had surely died away by then?'

'Not in my village. Don't look like that. I didn't suffer, because I was sent to live with my grandmother, the mountain witch, who could staunch the flow of blood. Everyone was afraid of her. How can I make her come alive for you?' Erika paused. 'Her name was Laila, a Sami name, or so the village people said. Actually, I'm sure she had Sami blood. Later a man visited a couple of times a year, in Sami dress. He was dour but loving too. One day I was told that this was my father.

'How can I describe Grandmother? She was as hard as a granite cliff but, unlike that, there was no time of year when she dressed up. There was nothing like the mountain-meadow flowers for her. But her vegetable patch was well kept.'

'The first important thing she taught me was to concentrate not on people's words when they spoke, but on their faces. So many people visited her. They came with their aching legs, their skin troubles and their haemorrhages. The consensus was that she could cure you. She always said that they cured themselves by their faith in her powers. She tested me each time someone had left the house. I had to remember what their faces had looked like while they were talking or complaining, how their changing expressions fitted with what they had said. She thought it crucial for me to practise this. She told me off for smiling too much and too willingly. She was really very angry and said she knew why I did it only too well.

'When Aunt Elin had brought me to the cottage the first time, there had been a row. Laila had said, through clenched teeth, that had she kept a calf as thin as this poor child, she would have gone blind with the shame of it.

' "You try then! See for yourself how easy it is to get that one to eat!" Aunt Elin screamed. "She's a spoilt brat." And I smiled.

' "Go away," Grandmother told her.

'Afterwards she gave me egg whisked with cream. Every day we talked about what we would eat for breakfast and supper. My mouth was always watering. Grandmother listened to me when I told her what kind of food I liked.

'Next, she taught me what the human body needs to grow tall and strong. "Not pickled herring," she said. Pickled herring made me vomit. "Now fresh fish, that's something else," she said. "Of course we'll eat fish, but so fresh it's still giving off water like steam."

'She taught me to fish. It was fun. When the fish bit, I burst out laughing. "That's how a smile should be," she said.

'She sleepwalked at night and soon I started to do it too. We would meet in the wild moonlit garden. We never spoke to each other then but that seemed perfectly normal to me. After all, we were each inside our own dream.

'We kept hens and I learnt to count by looking for their eggs and checking that they were all in the coop when I locked them up for the night. The fox would prowl after midnight, Grandmother said. She taught me to read, too. I had to know how, she said, because her own eyesight was weakening.

'She wasn't one for physical signs of affection, but she hugged me now and then. She would also say strange things, like "My daughter, at last". We must have loved each other, although we never used the word.

'She was religious. Not in the sense we mean. She didn't pray or sing hymns or go to church. She didn't use any of the usual God-speak either. You know what I mean – people will say things like, "What a divine day" when the sun's shining. But if April turned out as it should – pouring with rain in the morning, snowing by midday and blazing sun by evening – she would say, "Today God is looking after us." She really meant it, too.

'The weather watch we kept was special. I might be sitting on a rock, enjoying the stillness, the sun shining from a cloudless sky, but begin to feel a prickling on the skin of my arms. Then I would run to find Grandmother and tell her that soon there would be a storm. "Thought I felt it coming," she'd say. Then we set about getting the hens inside, and the cow too, and covering the lorry with a tarpaulin. We always finished just in time to be inside when the thunderstorm hit us and the rain poured down.

'I also developed the ability to know when the phone would ring. Grandmother laughed and said I was five minutes ahead of her. But, then, she could tell who was phoning and why. At times, she would look serious and say, "Something's up in the forest."

'During the autumn and winter forestry labourers swarmed all over the hillsides. Of course they had accidents. The axe would fall the wrong way and cut into a foot rather than a log. When this kind of thing happened, I knew what my tasks were: boil water, have a pile of clean linen cloths ready, get out the stretcher and so on. Everything must be just so by the time the lorry carrying the victim rolled into the yard in front of our cottage. Some cases were particularly bad, blood spurting in red shock-waves from the gaping wound. Even then Grandmother would have stopped it within a few minutes, briskly applied bandages, wrapped the man in thick blankets and transferred him to our lorry. I would sit with his head cradled in my lap and try to keep him calm as we drove down the steep mountain roads, along the river and into town, to hospital.

'Laila knew the doctor there. Every time he finished with a patient, he'd say to her, "Damn it, Laila, can't you tell me how you do it?"

' "How many times must I tell you? I don't know how I do it," she would reply.

'In the late summer of the year I was due to start school in the autumn, Grandmother was worried. Down at the estate farm it was taken for granted that I must "come home". It would not look good if I stayed away. Grandmother refused. I was sent to Social Services and put through a morning of questioning. I filled in a lot of forms too, which baffled them, because at the time the average seven-year-old couldn't read or write. They concluded that there was nothing wrong with my wits, or with my education. I was well-behaved too, polite and friendly. Then the doctor examined me and after tapping me all over my back and pinching and poking me, he pronounced that he had never seen a healthier child. They took a blood sample, which worried me. I wished Grandmother had been there. What if the bleeding wouldn't stop? In the end, they could find nothing wrong with me. Still, the lady who managed the local Social Services office was not satisfied. "The child's isolation must be taken into account."

'Grandmother used her old pick-up truck to solve the problem. She had it serviced in the garage and they fixed it, oiled it and replaced the worn parts. Then she drove me to the school gate every day and collected me in the afternoon. My other grandmother, my father's mother, said that this was unwise. Why wear yourself out so that a spoilt child can have its own way? Grandmother told her that there were many things beyond her understanding.

'I was never bullied, as they call it nowadays. Grandmother's special powers were well known in our area. On the other hand, no one wanted to be my friend so no one ever asked me to play. Later they showed openly how much they disliked me, probably because I did well at school. In a sense, that was due to cheating. Not that I realized it. But I knew the answers to all the questions and how to make the sums come out right without having to work at it. Put simply, I entered into our special world, Grandmother's and mine.

'What I did not know then, was that Grandmother had had a dream. She died on the day I passed my school-leaving exams. She had said in her will that all she owned should go to me, the cottage, the land and the money in her savings account. In an attached letter, she wrote that she saw me as a bridge between her knowledge and modern science. She wanted me to train in medicine.

'Now you know my story. That was how I was shaped. Now I feel tired and a little sad.'

27

When they were driving home in the twilight, Elisabeth sensed that Katarina was worried. 'What's the matter?' she asked.

Katarina banged her fist on the steering-wheel, so hard that the little car jumped. 'I'm determined to make Erika do what Laila wanted her to, damn it!'

'What was that?'

'Study medicine.'

'It's a long, hard course to follow. Erika has two children and a demanding husband to look after.'

'Olof isn't demanding, Mama, just spoilt. I'll sort him out.' She laughed and, for a second or so, was convinced that old Laila was winking to her from some star in the winter sky.

My headstrong daughter is back in control, Elisabeth thought. Oddly enough, this pleased her.

In the new house they went from room to room, delighted with what they saw. A big parcel was waiting for Elisabeth in the hall. She opened it and looked a little shamefaced. 'Gardening books,' she said. 'I ordered quite a few. And I've enrolled on a beginner's course in gardening.'

'That's a great idea!' Katarina said. She remembered the way Elisabeth had repeated, 'And a garden,' each time they had talked about the new house.

'Mama, I'll tell you what we'll do tomorrow,' she continued. 'We'll visit the woman who brought us the porridge. She said she was good with indoor plants, remember? I'll drive into town first and buy her a new one and then we'll call and wish her a happy new year or something.'

Elisabeth looked a little hesitant. She knew how tricky it might be to cope with an eager neighbour who had firm ideas on how a garden should look. On the other hand . . .

'She's reserved and when she laughs it sounds as if she had to take lessons in how to do it,' Katarina said, 'but I think a warm heart must be hidden behind that stiff façade.'

'Right you are. Let's go visiting.'

A couple of hours later, they went to bed in their separate flats. Elisabeth was finishing a thriller. Katarina kept her hands on her belly to feel her baby kicking. She no longer thought of the life that was growing inside her as 'the shoot', but as 'my baby'. The little unknown even had a name. She was called Laila.

All went according to plan at the beginning of their visit to the porridge-woman, whose name was Ingrid. She seemed genuinely pleased when they arrived and amazed when Katarina called, 'Let me in quickly or this miracle bloom will get frost damage!'

It was an azalea, almost a metre tall and covered in ripe flower buds. 'Goodness me, you mustn't, that's so expensive . . .' Ingrid stuttered helplessly.

Ingrid's house suited its owner, Katarina thought. It was straightforward, honest, with hardly any decorative objects like souvenirs or candlesticks. Instead there were massed banks of plants on wide benches in front of all the windows.

The large table in the middle of the sitting-room was covered with catalogues and information on plants. A thousand colourful blooms, on shrubs, annuals and perennials, glowed against the background of the dark oak tabletop.

Elisabeth, who was usually punctiliously well-mannered, sank immediately on to a chair and began to leaf through some of the brochures. 'This is fantastic!' she exclaimed.

'It's very seductive,' Ingrid said.

'I'd love to be seduced,' Elisabeth replied, and Ingrid smiled her reluctant smile and said that this was indeed a time of year for nurturing dreams.

Katarina and Elisabeth exchanged a surprised glance. Then they turned to look out of the window. Outside, the orchard trees were battered by the wind, the snow flurries were thick and the temperature twenty-two degrees below.

'I've read about you in the paper,' Ingrid said, and looked at Elisabeth. 'You're a scholar, with a doctorate.'

'It's no use to anyone,' Elisabeth said.

Katarina smiled. 'My mother understands the art of speaking,' she said to Ingrid. 'She's seductive too, in a way, when she writes and lectures. She can make all kinds of contradictory ideas merge into theories that stimulate your imagination.'

Elisabeth nodded thoughtfully. 'You know what they say, Ingrid. Out of the mouths of fools and children . . .' That reminded her of Jack O'Hara, but she did not understand why.

'So how come you're suddenly so interested in gardening, Dr Elg?'

There was no sarcasm in the question and Elisabeth took it at face value. When she started to explain, her answer became more personal than she had planned. 'We must be about the same age, so I'm sure you, too, remember how it used to be: the dream of having your own home – a small house, prettily furnished and perfectly looked after, something to be proud of. It would prove that you had been successful in life. Isn't that how you remember it?'

'Yes, it is. Most of us failed, though, one way or another. The children arrived and with them came toys and clutter, dirty nappies and crumbs. And constant tiredness.'

'That's right. Always being tired.' Elisabeth paused for a while. Then she started speaking again. 'My husband was a wife-beater. He hit me until all my dreams had gone. Without them I became a nobody and everything around me fell apart.' Again, she paused. 'When I occasionally emerged from my . . . paralysis . . . I tried to be interested in the garden. I would potter about, dig and sow, but nothing ever grew properly. The garden became a symbol of how I failed in everything I undertook.'

Another long pause. Elisabeth concluded, 'So when my daughter suggested that we should buy a house together, the thought of a garden seemed a wonderful opportunity. The baby would enjoy it too. It could play among the flowers.'

For the first time since they had started talking together, Ingrid seemed eager to join in. 'Nothing is as rewarding as seeing a seed take root and grow into a plant, or a bud flower,' she said. 'Except seeing a child grow, of course,' she added, and her voice faltered.

This was when Elisabeth asked the fateful question: 'Do you have any children?'

'I did,' Ingrid replied. 'They died in a plane accident. In the Alps. They were twins, boys, nineteen years old.'

The silence was deafening, impenetrable. Ingrid broke it. 'My husband died soon afterwards. He lost the will to live . . . He shot himself.'

Katarina searched for support from her mother, but Elisabeth did not look at her. Her fists were clenched, the knuckles white. Then she spread out her fingers, made fists again, repeated the gesture. Spreading, clenching – Katarina recognized it. This was what her mother had done on Friday nights, when she expected her husband home.

Katarina looked down at her own hands. They were shaking.

Ingrid said, in a tone of polite enquiry, 'Now I'm sure you'd all like a cup of coffee?'

'No, thank you, but a cold drink would be lovely.'

'Yes, of course. Would you like some mint-flavoured white-currant juice?'

She disappeared into the kitchen. The silence when she returned with the tray burdened them all. Her guests did not dare look at each other, Katarina had paled and Elisabeth was in tears.

Ingrid looked embarrassed. 'You must think me very hard, the way I threw my past into your faces. It's just that I thought it would be better coming from me, rather than on the grapevine.'

They nodded.

'Everyone knows and the way I'm constantly pitied makes me feel . . . tired. When people come face to face with someone else's catastrophe it frightens them. They want to run away. Please don't be offended, but it's impossible for outsiders to understand . . . well, whatever. No one can.' She sat in silence for a while. 'My past opened an abyss between me and everyone else.'

Elisabeth came over to sit next to her on the sofa. She tried to take Ingrid's hand, but Ingrid wouldn't let her. She sat there dry-eyed and stiff, suddenly hard as stone.

They would never remember how they managed to say goodbye and leave, but always how the wind turned their tears to ice before they reached their own house.

28

Early next morning the telephone rang. It was Viktor Emmanuel, who wanted to remind Katarina of her promise to model for him. 'Today!' he said.

'This isn't day, it's night.'

'So it hasn't occurred to you that dark's the order of the day at this time of the year? It's past eight o'clock. The kids are already stuck into their schoolwork.'

Katarina giggled and muttered something.

'What's that?'

'I said, I'm coming. Give me half an hour.'

The battle for the Line started.

Katarina was given a long grey outfit with a hood, and perched on the edge of a folding bed with a pile of cushions to lean on. She had to get used to the strong light, reflected back from the white wall behind her.

Viktor Emmanuel was chasing the right line on the huge sheets of his drawing pad. Again and again he failed, swore, scratched his head, tore off yet another sheet and moaned in agony. After a while he was up to his knees in discarded sketches. Katarina thought she heard him sob at one point. She relaxed when he started swearing again.

The hours passed.

In spite of her relatively comfortable position, Katarina began to feel weary. 'I must move around a bit.'

'Why?'

'I've got cramp in my left leg.'

'Forget it. Let me try just once more.'

Elisabeth arrived and liberated them both. She had brought sandwiches. 'How's it going?'

'Piss awful. Just rubbish, the whole fucking thing.'

Elisabeth always listened to and tried to understand everyone. Including madmen. 'What are you after?' she asked.

'THE LINE!' he roared.

He kicked the pile of discarded paper, took Elisabeth's hand and made her slide it along Katarina's body. 'Can't you feel it? The line. It's the line that goes from the boiling hot interior of the earth straight up to God.'

He tore his hair and groaned. Like the Old Testament Jews, Elisabeth thought.

'I can't draw it. Can't. Do you see it?'

Passion always frightened her. She shook her head. 'No, Viktor, I'm so sorry. I don't see anything special.'

This silenced him, but only for a moment. 'If you can't see it, you who've had children, then you must see how important it is that I catch the line and show it to the world.'

Katarina had got up to stretch her legs. Her shadow fell on the brightly lit wall behind her and suddenly Elisabeth saw a long, soft line, the swelling caused by the unknown life inside her daughter's body. 'Viktor Emmanuel, I think I do see after all.'

They were silent, all three of them.

Then Katarina said, 'What about a cup of coffee?'

Blessed normality took over. They laughed, switched off the lamps and wandered out into the kitchen.

The next day the battle for the Line started afresh.

Katarina came early to sit. Viktor was still damp after his shower. While he was rubbing his hair dry, he said, sounding a little ashamed, 'I hope I didn't make you go off me with my tantrums yesterday, Katarina.'

'Please, don't be silly. You're one of those people who're serious about what they do and that's the kind of person I like best.'

They started again and soon he was tearing at his hair in desperation once more. The baby must have sensed the tension because, in the middle of the session, she started kicking like never before. 'Viktor Emmanuel, please come here. Hurry,' Katarina called.

For a long time he knelt in front of her with his hand on her belly, feeling the kicking until the little one went back to sleep.

Then he rose. His eyes were half closed. 'Maybe . . . it may just be that . . . I've captured the feel of it,' he said. 'We'll carry on tomorrow. I've got too much on my mind now.'

'That's fine.'

Katarina went home. She boiled two eggs and peeled a hundred grams of fresh prawns. She shared the food with her mother.

Next morning, at eight forty-three, he caught the Line. He was not jubilant then, just gripped with quiet awe.

29

One day just after Katarina had got back from work Ingrid phoned and asked if it was all right for her to call and show them some photographs.

Elisabeth, who had been studying gardening books all day, was pleased at the interruption. 'You're welcome. I look forward to seeing you.'

Ingrid spread out her pictures. 'I wanted to start with the most beautiful garden in the whole area. It belongs to our crazy artist. People call him lazy, but that's wrong. There's hardly anything that's more difficult to achieve in a garden than establishing a wildflower meadow and keeping it going.'

Elisabeth took in the spring pictures: snowdrops, drifts of white anemones. Later, bluebells formed a carpet in many shades of blue. Summer brought wild and cultivated poppies in profusion, delicate field bluebells, armfuls of cornflowers mixed with yellow buttercups and white and yellow marguerites. 'That's how I would like my garden,' she said.

'I wouldn't,' Katarina said. 'I don't want to be out there scything the grass all the time. I don't want to have to leave dry seed pods in place and keep checking that the soil is suitably sandy and poor.'

'It's extraordinary how knowledgeable you've become all of a sudden,' Elisabeth said tartly.

'Come off it, Mama, architects have to have some knowledge of gardening. For instance, I might have to cover up – "shrub up", we call it – a misshapen front elevation.'

She laughed, Ingrid tried out her dry cackle, but Elisabeth was still cross. 'If you know so much, maybe you could produce some ideas for our garden. I haven't heard you make a single suggestion.'

'But you're making it. I'm supposed to give birth soon. It's called a division of labour. Let's try it out now: you two stay here and plan the garden. I'll fix some coffee for my brother. He's on his way over for a private chat with me.'

'Why don't you use my sitting room upstairs?' Elisabeth said, and smiled.

Katarina, who had felt a little anxious about how her mother would respond, thought that she might have an idea of what Olof wanted to discuss.

A quarter of an hour later Olof arrived. He kicked off his boots in the hall, hugged his mother and greeted Ingrid politely.

Katarina rushed downstairs and gave him a welcoming kiss. 'I've fixed some coffee for us. Come upstairs and leave these two in peace to plan gardens. OK?'

Elisabeth looked at them, her children. She felt happy and proud, until she met Ingrid's eyes. Then, she remembered, and was ashamed.

Upstairs, Olof settled at Elisabeth's desk. Katarina curled up like a cat in the old sofa.

'The phone rang in the middle of the night, just before Christmas,' Olof began. 'The caller was an American lawyer. It was two thirty in the morning, and I had to speak English.

'Her message – the lawyer was a woman – was that Jack O'Hara was suicidal. He had just been released from a police cell where he had been kept after a drunken fight. His father got him out, but he had disappeared again. While he was staying with his family, he had told them about a Swedish girl he had fallen in love with. And then had almost killed.'

'Olof, what am I supposed to do about this?'

'You're not meant to do anything. I came to an arrangement with the lawyer: Jack would phone me at any time, night or day, when he turned up again. He did, and this time I was better prepared. I taped our conversation and you can listen to it now.'

Katarina listened. Her eyes grew dark, but her face was very still. 'Please play it again,' she said, when the tape ended.

He nodded, rewound it, then the voices spoke again.

In the end, Katarina almost screamed, 'He's blaming me.'

'Please, don't be so silly. He's taking responsibility for his own life – whatever he gets up to . . . beating up women or driving under the influence in New York. The reason I agreed to listen to him at all was because of your child, Katarina.'

'Who has a right to know who her father is. As Mama keeps telling me.'

'That's right.'

'Yes, it is. You're right, both of you. There must be some way I can deal with this, with Jack. Oh, I know I should, I know.' She wept. 'But, Olof, please understand, I'm paralysed somehow over him. About everything that happened. About having been in love with him.'

Olof nodded. 'I'll go downstairs and chat to Mama while you work out what you want to do.'

'No, wait. I already know. We must do what you think is right: we'll invite the whole lot of them over from the USA for the christening.'

'Great,' Olof said. When he left the room, he heard her laugh. She sounded close to tears.

In the downstairs sitting room, Ingrid and Elisabeth had agreed on a long order for seeds from an English nursery. 'Lots of wonderful seeds,' Elisabeth said, beaming with satisfaction.

Ingrid rose. She said she had to go home.

Olof accompanied her to the door. 'I shall look forward to seeing you again soon,' he told her. Then he said to his mother, 'Katarina will explain what all this was about.'

'She's crying, isn't she?'

'Yes, she is,' Olof replied. 'Guilty conscience' was written all over his face. 'But you will be pleased.'

He called upstairs before he left, ''Bye! And, Katarina, one of us must phone . . .'

'Please, you do it . . . please.'

'I promise.'

They were alone at last. Katarina smiled through her tears at her mother. 'Mama, it's time to get that bottle of brandy out.'

'But, darling, should you . . . ?'

'Just a sip.'

While Elisabeth enjoyed the calming drink, her daughter told her of the phone call from the American lawyer. Then she ran the tape.

Elisabeth listened to it twice, just as her daughter had. 'Katarina, what will you do?'

'We'll invite them to the christening.'

Before they said goodnight, Katarina said, 'You always insisted that when things became as bad as they ever were, you found yourself unable to act. Paralysed. I never quite understood what it was like. Not until now, when I realize that's exactly what happened to me after Jack hit me. I didn't want to remember, I didn't want to understand or even think about him. Definitely not act. If you do, somehow the whole thing becomes more real. But now I must act.'

30

The miracle of spring was taking place in Sweden. The ice broke up and the snow covering the roofs turned to streams of water.

Spring had arrived earlier in New York. It rained, and spring flowers grew in the parks, but Jack found it hard to breathe the mixture of rain and exhaust fumes. He was getting ready to go to California and deal with the divorce proceedings. Initially, he had thought it would be straightforward: admit guilt, agree to everything and hand over his inheritance from his grandfather to Grace and the children. There was nothing to fear: he should simply make an honest effort to tidy up the mess he had created.

But now that the day had drawn close, it seemed less simple. He felt frightened.

Reluctantly, he saw that this had a lot to do with having confided in Ed and Janet. And in Olof Elg.

'The more you talk about these things, the worse they get,' he said to Janet.

She agreed that he wasn't entirely wrong, but added, 'Still, by speaking about one's feelings, they become brute reality rather than threatening ghosts – and that's got to be good. Reality is better than fantasy any time.'

It was Sunday and as usual they had stayed at the breakfast table.

'Why did you marry Grace?' Ed asked. 'It was obvious from the start that she . . . had problems. Mentally.'

'Dad, I was in love, crazy about her. Sad women do something to me, always have.'

'Something about wanting to be the comforter . . . ?'

Jack's wry smile lit up his face. His eyes gleamed with irony when he said, 'Making it with a woman in despair and getting her to feel good – better – has always turned me on sexually.'

Janet said nothing. Jack noticed that she was not looking at him and was avoiding Ed's eyes too. She seemed to be watching something interesting above their heads. Then she took her eyes off the ceiling and asked, 'What does Grace want by way of alimony?'

'Everything. I'll agree to it, of course.'

'Everything?'

'I've got a letter from her lawyers. Hang on, I'll go and get it.'

It was a long document. Janet went into her office with it while Ed started to clear the table and load the breakfast things into the dishwasher.

Jack saw that his father's hands were shaking. 'It's only money,' he said. 'It'll be over soon and then I'm free.'

'Yeah? And then what?'

Suddenly, Jack felt he could talk about the book he was planning.

'Get this, Dad. I was lecturing at this place in Sweden. They call it a summer university but it's nice 'n' easy. There are no exams, no points to score. Students and teachers are relaxed and I felt I could . . . spread my wings. I speculated, let scientific evidence go hang, drew mad but intellectually interesting parallels between the practices and beliefs of Indian shamans and Celtic Druids. I chased the cult of the Great Mother from one cultural setting to the next and got into the story of the Germanic tribes, like how they arrived in Europe and from where. I always took care to say it was mostly speculation, though obviously I had quite a few facts to base it on, linguistic ones mainly.'

Jack was enthused and when he saw that Ed was interested, he added, 'I'm not boasting but my summer lectures in Stockholm went down well. In the evenings I began to think about writing a book on popular science.'

'Brilliant idea,' Janet said. She had been standing in the doorway, listening. Ed beamed with delight.

'There's just one problem,' Jack said. 'I'm putting my academic reputation on the line.'

'You want to know my opinion? Forget your academic reputation!' Ed declared.

'I'm hearing you,' Jack said, and laughed.

He started to tell them more, then went to get his lecture notes and illustrations. They asked questions and Jack responded eloquently.

The early part of the day passed quickly and pleasantly. Ed was fascinated by Jack's ideas and Janet by the way Jack had come alive, his personality sparkling through.

The conversation continued over lunch in the kitchen. 'What are you waiting for?' Ed asked. 'You seem to have it all set up and ready to go.'

'I thought I'd wait until the divorce was out of the way,' Jack explained. 'There's a lot planning and thinking to do, like crafting coherent outlines for chapters and settling on the content. It's quite a lot of work.'

'Speaking of your divorce, you and I will sift through Grace's demands,' Janet said. 'She's hired a good lawyer, Jack. You need one too. I'll do your pleading, if you like.'

'No fee bargaining, though, I'll pay you in full,' Jack said.

'Jack, it's not just a matter of money. It's about your reputation and good name. And, the bottom line, your self-confidence.'

When Ed went off to take a nap, Jack and Janet withdrew into her office and settled down at her large desk.

'Have you actually read the Californian lawyer's letter?' she asked.

'Just skimmed it. I'd made up my mind to agree to everything from the start.'

'She's accusing you of having abused her. Jack, is that true?'

'Yes.'

Janet did not look into his eyes. Once more she seemed fascinated by the ceiling. He observed her without blushing or fidgeting.

Has he no shame? she thought, and asked, 'How can you beat up someone who's mentally ill?'

'You must try to understand what it was like when she was sinking deeper and deeper. I was hanging on to her but she slipped away, out of my grasp. There was nothing I could do. I was helpless, tried to shake her into clarity but it didn't bring her back.

'Was she "mentally ill"? I never understood about that. Later, a doctor told me she was a manic-depressive. It was an illness, he said. The depressive phases would come and go. It meant that her state of mind wasn't my fault and that was a relief to me. The doc kept saying so . . . He said I mustn't blame myself.

'But, of course, it also meant I wasn't responsible for the periods when she was full of zest for life. It was just another automatic response. She took these tablets that seemed to cut out her biggest mood swings, but by then I was past caring. I ran away . . .'

Janet sat in silence. Jack got up and started to pace. 'I loved her, you know. She was so alive, so vibrant.'

'Love is a diffuse word. I don't like it. Maybe you loved her because you had power over her.'

He did not answer and she stared at the ceiling. 'You admit that you "shook her" to bring her back to reality. You never hit her, then?'

'I can't remember.'

'Good, that's the line we'll take. You were desperate and had some childish notion that you could get her to face reality by giving her a good shake.' Janet wrote a long report to the San Francisco legal firm. She reduced the huge sum Grace was demanding in alimony. Even then it would be expensive for Jack. He had the right to see his children, she told him. She thought this was important, but Jack said he would never use it.

The divorce itself was a formality.

31

That year spring did not come in its usual slow, uncertain way, hesitating before each phase. No, it came like a tidal wave. Rain sheeted down, day and night, as if the sky had opened the floodgates. The grey snow vanished and the roads, meadows and woodland paths ran with muddy water. Both radio and TV broadcast incessant reports of misery; Lake Vänern burst its banks and rising water threatened the quays in the many harbour towns on Sweden's long coasts.

Katarina and Elisabeth took all this calmly and spent their evenings in front of the burning logs in the fireplace, listening to the rain. It hammered against the windows, driven by squally spring winds.

Viktor Emmanuel wandered in and out, as had become his habit. He always accepted a beer and said he enjoyed the wet, violent spring. 'I've always been attracted to disasters.'

Katarina nodded and admitted that she felt the same.

Elisabeth snorted irritably.

Ingrid called, bearing the seed packets they had ordered from England. 'Our gardens are in an awful mess just now,' she said. 'We'll have to start the seeds inside.'

The downpour lasted six days and six nights. On the seventh day, the sun rose bright and round. They watched this miracle of nature through the kitchen window.

'It's like the passage in Genesis, remember: "On the seventh day . . ."?' Katarina had long since forgotten what happened on the seventh day. 'Was that the day God separated heaven from earth?'

'No, surely not. Wait, I'll go and look it up.'

Elisabeth came back with the Old Testament, laughing. 'Ha, that was the day when He rested.'

A few hours later the air was warm, and steam rose from the

damp soil. A week or so later, coltsfoot and blue anemones were in full bloom.

Spring seemed to be striding irresistibly ahead.

Ingrid said, 'Believe me, this can't last. We'll pay for it.'

But spring did not retreat. The sun kept shining, the earth gave off moisture and warmed.

'Bloody good planning,' Viktor Emmanuel said. 'This way, the frost will be gone from the soil in a few days.'

This pleased Elisabeth so much that she made a delicious fish pie and invited the artist for supper.

They sat at the table long after they had eaten. The blue spring twilight was gathering and darkening around them. Elisabeth took her courage in both hands and asked how he had come to be such a 'man apart'.

His wooden face creased with thought. 'I find words difficult, unlike you.'

Suddenly he began to tell the story of his childhood. His mother had produced six children within ten years. She had married at twenty and at thirty-two, she had all these children. She had found it hard to get a moment to herself or a chance to talk to one child alone. 'We weren't poverty-stricken, ours was a decent artisan's home. But, of course, it was hard to make ends meet.' His eyes wandered, lost among the images of childhood. Then he sighed. 'At first she raged against fate when she became pregnant again at the age of forty. I was her late baby.'

He laboured to explain how extraordinary it had been for him to receive all of the maternal love she had not been able to give to her other children. Now all her time and interest, on which the others had missed out, was focused on her youngest. Stored love had been waiting for him, like capital in a savings account. 'Ready to be paid out, with interest.'

He described their walks in the countryside around their house and how they would stop to look at every insect, worm or plant. She could tell him about all these things. 'If there was something she didn't know, we'd go to the library together and look it up,' he said. He laughed at the memory of how they had sat in the silent reading room, a middle-aged woman and a little boy, deep in study and surrounded by piles of reference books on flora and fauna. He remembered a big illustrated volume on trees. 'I'm trying to tell you how I became someone who sees.'

'Is that why you go to visit her most weekends? She's still alive, isn't she?' Katarina asked.

'She's very much alive. I know no one else like her.'

Elisabeth brought him back to his account of himself by asking if he had developed a particular way of viewing the world because he had 'learnt to see' so early in life.

'You put it so well,' he said, looking self-conscious. 'A world-view, now. I don't know.'

Elisabeth looked disappointed.

'Forgive me,' he said. 'You must understand that I don't trust words. I have only a limited supply and I'm afraid to use them. It's so easy to change reality by pronouncing on this and that, stating opinions.'

'But how can we deal with reality? And where is it?'

He thought about this. 'Reality is . . . in the mind, first of all. We know what our senses tell us. We see the sun rising from the sea, red and round, and the moon hanging like a silver plate in the sky at night. To the child, the twinkling stars wink as if hinting at a shared secret. Then there's a second reality, which we know about through studying. We learn that the sun is a star on fire and the moon a lump of rock circling our planet. And our earth is nothing but a small member of an unbelievably large population of planets in an infinite universe.'

'Do you think we've lost wisdom by embracing knowledge? As T. S. Eliot says in that poem of his – do you know it?'

Katarina smiled. Viktor Emmanuel thought again before he answered.

'There's a third way of seeing reality, a quite different way.'

'Do you mean mystics have a view of reality too?'

'I don't care much for that word. What I meant is not at all mystical, something hidden or lost in the mist. It's more like something you can learn. And then this connection with the world becomes a . . . an intellectual experience.'

The other two were silent while they tried to understand what he meant.

'Remember the Line?' Viktor asked.

'When Katarina was sitting for you and you were tearing your hair in desperation?'

'Yes. You didn't understand what I was after at first. Then, when Katarina stood up, her shadow fell on the wall behind her and there was the Line – or, at least, you drew a breath and said you understood.'

'Are you telling me that I was in touch with the third level of reality?'

But at that point Viktor got up, thanked them for the meal and said goodnight. And added, looking touchingly embarrassed, that they were to take no notice of him, he'd been talking too much.

32

The next morning the sun shone over the land – yet another sunny morning! By the afternoon, clusters of light clouds had gathered in the sky. Elisabeth said that maybe Ingrid would be proved right: now they would have to pay for the lovely spring days.

Later, the clouds dissolved easily, like dreams, and the sky glowed more intensely blue than before.

Elisabeth went off to catch a train – she was going to a lecture at the university. Thankfully, the train stopped right in front of the great complex of buildings at Frescati.

Katarina had decided to visit Viktor Emmanuel, who was sorting out his studio.

'Hi,' she said. Suddenly she felt shy and blushed as she tried to find the right words. 'I wanted to tell you how grateful I am for what you told us yesterday. It was the first time I understood that art could be . . . the path to the third level of reality.'

'One path, yes. There are many. One – and a very common one – is religion. Sadly, most religions turn symbols and myths into historical reality.'

'Which is playing absurd games with reality,' Katarina said.

'Who said that?'

'I think you did, once. Or maybe my mother.'

Viktor Emmanuel laughed and Katarina smiled.

'But I wanted to ask you one more thing. What do you think love is?'

'Love between two human beings?'

'Yes. You've had a long, happy marriage and must know something about it.'

'It is about being two interconnected vessels.'

She closed her eyes and thought of Jack. With him, even ordinary conversation had been impossible at times. I must have been crazy, she thought. It was like an illness. All that time, her need for new men.

At the next moment she realized that the atmosphere between her and the artist was vibrating with tension. She looked at the large, heavy figure in front of her. Her nipples grew hard and hot, she felt damp between her legs.

'Come,' he said, lifted her in his arms and carried her to his bed. They came together gently, with tenderness and desire. He did not enter her, did not invade the nest where the baby slept, but touched and caressed her until she reached orgasm. She did the same for him.

They fell asleep afterwards. When she woke, she stroked his beard and said that this was yet another way to reach the third level of reality.

He muttered in agreement.

They did not do it again, restrained both by her big belly and his fear of hurting her. They did not talk about their encounter but exchanged many glances as the days passed and spring moved through April. Soon it would be May.

There were so many thoughts for her to examine and re-examine. Most often, they concerned her past. My obsession with sex, she said to herself, always falling in love, always chasing men and using them for entertainment – what was it all about?

When the birches were covered in tiny green leaves and it was time to prune the roses, Viktor Emmanuel drove a small lorry along the track leading up the slope along the backs of the gardens. Ingrid, in fighting mood, was sitting next to him. The lorry was laden with boulders. Some were huge, some medium-sized, but most were small and round.

'Elisabeth, it's about time you had a real hillside in your garden, not that excuse for a rockery. We'll have to wait for Olof because we need more men. I've phoned him.'

Katarina left for her last day at work. She had been moaning about it to her mother. 'They're excluding me from all the big, exciting projects and giving me piddling little things. I know why – I'll be on maternity leave for a year. But, still, I'm not very happy about it. It's as if I've lost my professional competence because I'm going to have a baby.'

'It's called the women's trap. You're caught in it, and will have to put up with the consequences.'

Katarina said goodbye to her colleagues at work and was relieved to get home. She was not surprised when she spotted the lorry at the back of their house. 'You knew about this,' Elisabeth exclaimed.

'Of course I did, Mama. This is your birthday present from your children and your friends here. Have you forgotten you'll be sixty soon?'

'When I celebrate my birthday we'll be in another world,' Elisabeth said. 'The world of a new baby.'

The plumber arrived – in a construction worker's hat. He had brought Olof too. They were each given a bottle of beer and then they got started.

There was no question about who was in charge: Viktor Emmanuel decided how and where the stones would be arranged. He took them through a day's tough work with military precision. He roared orders to his subordinates and they beavered away, shifting the boulders into place.

Then they were allowed another beer, and after that they had to put the smaller stones in place. The artist was still leading his troops, roaring and swearing if the pebbles ended up in the wrong crevice or, worse still, piled up into a little mountain.

'Bloody hell, can't you see? You're fucking up the entire structure.'

Ingrid was the most accurate stone-thrower.

Later Viktor and Olof shared a shower and Olof at last mustered the courage to say something to Viktor that he had wanted to voice for a long time. 'I was in London at a conference some time ago. Most of the others joined a guided tour on the free afternoon, but I went to a gallery where you had an exhibition on. I had read about you in the Swedish newspapers and was curious about your work.' They dried themselves on huge towels. Olof tried to find the right words to tell Viktor what he had felt. He failed, and simply said, 'I felt I had seen God at work.'

Viktor Emmanuel hid his face in the towel. Eventually, he muttered, 'Bloody hell. My dear lad. You couldn't have made me happier.'

Elisabeth and Ingrid spent the next few days filling in the crevices in the new rockery with soil. Viktor Emmanuel carried on ordering everyone about. 'Large ferns, there. Hosta, variegated, there. On the sloping sides thyme, fine ground cover, good colour in the summer, lovely smell. Next year you can try annuals.'

Katarina called on him and said that it was time to settle the bill. She and Olof would pay what they owed.

Viktor Emmanuel told her they would have to wait. 'You see, I'm going away for while.'

'For how long?'

He saw the anxiety in her face and hid his pleasure. 'Just for a week, no more.'

'Where are you going?'

'To New York. Ingrid is coming with me to keep me in order. I'm going to sell my triptych to the Museum of Modern Art.'

Katarina shouted with delight, so loudly that Elisabeth came downstairs. By then, her daughter was already in Viktor's arms. But it was just a friendly hug – their bellies prevented any more.

'Mama, you must hear this! The Museum of Modern Art in New York is going to buy Viktor's triptych. I'm so happy, so proud to be your friend,' she said, and beat on his chest with her fists.

'Oh, my God,' Elisabeth said. She had to sit down. 'Millions of people will see it. It's wonderful news.'

Viktor Emmanuel laughed, a little embarrassed. 'Actually, I

didn't want to sell, but they offered me such an enormous sum for it.'

Then they shook hands and said things like 'Have a good time' and 'Take care' and 'Come back soon'.

That night, in the kitchen, Katarina asked, 'Do you understand why Ingrid is travelling with him?'

'She manages his accounts. Well, actually all his business dealings. She prices his paintings when he's selling, organizes his exhibitions and sees to it that he pays his taxes when they're due. She's a trained arts administrator and used to work for a legal firm before the twins were born.'

Elisabeth went on to tell her how, just a week after Ingrid's life had fallen apart, Viktor Emmanuel had called on her to ask for her help.

33

Easter had come and gone. The next week was quiet in the house at Oxel Street. Elisabeth and Katarina missed their neighbours, Viktor Emmanuel and Ingrid.

But the phone kept ringing, as it had since they moved in.

Almost all the calls were for Elisabeth. Her many friends in Gävle wanted to know how she was and tell her how they were. They told her about their children, their jobs and the books they had read – wanting to talk themselves out, as Elisabeth put it.

Now and then there was a call for Katarina, but usually from her colleagues in the office who had been unable to locate a drawing or a memo.

One afternoon when Katarina was resting, she steeled herself to consider why she had no friends. She had enjoyed the social round of the big city. She was good-looking and easy to talk to, a popular guest with a steady stream of invitations to parties and receptions. But friendship was different. Did she have a close rapport even with one person, someone she could trust? No, she did not.

Suddenly a wine-bar conversation came back to her: she had told a woman that 'Learning new things to do in bed is my idea of a good time'. And her acquaintance had replied that she felt sorry for Katarina.

Now she blushed. I talked about sex all the time, she thought. Why? Where did the need come from, and where did it drive me?

Into Jack's arms. 'Changing men the way normal women change panties,' he had shouted at her. Everyone knew, he had told her. Had 'everyone' in her circle really been saying these things? Yes, she could almost hear the whispers: 'She's man-mad, watch out.'

She sat bolt upright in bed and said aloud, 'It isn't true. I never chased married men.'

Then she recalled that Jack was married, with two children.

'I didn't mean any harm,' she whimpered.

It sounded feeble.

Her conscience told her that she had been selfish. Some men behaved in that way, usually immature men whom she despised.

Her baby kicked. She put her hand on her belly and suddenly remembered her thoughts as she had been driving along the river Ljusnan. She had been looking out over it when she told herself, 'I'm afraid of becoming too close to someone.'

When Elisabeth arrived with a cup of tea, and saw that Katarina had been crying, 'Tell me, dear heart,' she said.

'I was asking myself why I've no friends and you have so many.' Then Katarina could talk about the need for sex that had driven her, the gossip and even what Jack had said.

Elisabeth listened. As ever, she uttered not a word of comfort, but Katarina felt better.

The next day Erika and her new friend Ulla were coming over. They would not be bringing their children and sounded as elated as freed prisoners.

'Would you cook? I'm feeling a bit tired,' Elisabeth said.

Katarina felt a stab of anxiety. Before he had left, Viktor Emmanuel had told her he was concerned about Elisabeth. 'Keep an eye on her. She's abnormally tired, it seems to me. She should have a thorough medical check-up.'

Katarina had given him a list of psychological reasons for the tiredness: moving house, the new environment, leaving a lifetime's work. Maybe worrying about the baby . . .

'That's rubbish. Mentally, Elisabeth is A1. Not physically, though. I suspect something's wrong.'

He had sounded serious.

Katarina mixed the pastry dough for a salmon pie, and drove off to get the ingredient for the filling: salmon, prawns, thick cream. She stopped off at the clinic and saw her midwife, Birgitta.

'What brings you here?'

'Nothing to do with me, but I'm worried about my mother. I

just wondered if you could recommend a doctor she could see at the health centre?' She described Elisabeth's constant tiredness.

'I'll arrange an appointment for her with Robert Gille and phone to let you know.'

On the way home, Katarina thought about what she saw as her close relationship with Birgitta. It held an element of true friendship, even though that might have been down to the midwife's professionalism. Probably all expectant mothers were made to feel that. Still, what mattered was that Katarina herself had sensed the warmth and could accept it without reservation.

This is new, she thought. Then: My baby did this for me.

While she was unpacking the groceries, the phone rang. I'll say that Mama's resting and will call back later, she thought.

It was Erika. She couldn't get away because both boys had gastric flu and the doctor was expected at any minute. 'I'm so sorry . . .' she said.

Katarina felt unreasonably disappointed. She pulled herself together and asked, almost humbly, if Ulla might like to come out to see them anyway.

'Why don't you ask her? I'll find her number.'

Ulla sounded pleased. 'Of course I'd love to come. I'm looking forward to meeting you.'

And I need someone to talk to, Katarina thought. Aloud she said, 'Me too. Great!'

With only two to feed, she decided to make two small pies and keep one for another day. These days Elisabeth picked at her food like a bird.

Katarina was peeling prawns in the kitchen when she heard Elisabeth's uncertain, slow steps on the stairs. Another stab of fear struck her. It was impossible to doubt that something was wrong. Why hadn't she been more alert?

'Let me do that,' Elisabeth said. She carried on peeling the prawns while Katarina chopped dill, cleaned the salmon and prepared the sauce.

'Erika can't come. The boys are in bed, ill.'

'It's not serious, is it?' Elisabeth's voice shook.

'No, not at all. Ulla's coming anyway.'

'That's nice. Oh, I've got another piece of good news. Ingrid called. She and Viktor are flying into Arlanda tomorrow afternoon.'

Relief flowed through Katarina in a great wave. She could not hide her feelings, did not even try to when she said, 'Thank God for that. I'm so pleased.'

The telephone rang again. This time it was Birgitta. Dr Gille had agreed to see Mrs Elg at eleven o'clock on Monday. 'There's a long waiting list for his surgery but he agreed to make an exception for Mrs Elg.'

'Thank you very much for your help.'

'Mama, you must listen to me. I've arranged an appointment for you at the health centre on Monday morning. The doctor was recommended to me, and he's kind and competent.'

She was prepared for protests but Elisabeth agreed without a murmur. 'I must find out why I'm so tired.'

Katarina's mind whispered: Cancer. But no, surely not that. Her hands shook as she stirred the sauce.

Ulla looked like a rosy-cheeked little girl. Everything about her was soft and childish, her pouting mouth, small snub nose and round blue eyes, which always seemed wide with astonishment. However, it soon became clear that she was highly intelligent.

Ulla did all the talking and laughing over lunch. She told amusing family stories about her plumber husband and their three boys. Katarina felt she should contribute but could not think of anything to say. Elisabeth laughed several times while she pushed a tiny helping of the food around her plate.

After lunch she went upstairs to lie down.

'How long has she been like this?'

'It's hard to say because it's come over her so slowly. You must have met her many times at Erika's.'

Ulla nodded. 'She has changed a great deal.' She hesitated a little then continued, 'My mother had breast cancer. They operated on both her breasts and took out a lot of lymph nodes. She had radiotherapy afterwards and now she's cured. She only has check-ups a couple of times a year.'

The tension in Katarina eased.

'I can't deny that it was an awful time,' Ulla said. 'Like you, I was expecting my first baby.'

'Oh, God.'

Ulla paused. Then she said, 'I was the only child of a single mother. She was great, gave me everything I needed . . .'

Katarina made coffee and they carried their mugs into the sitting room. Then Katarina confided in Ulla. She spoke of how she had chased men, always looking for new erotic experiences. All the time she was haunted by the thought that she shouldn't be saying this, that Ulla would be disgusted . . .

'I recognize what you're telling me,' Ulla said. 'I was just like that when I was young. Well, until I met Lars, and by then I was well over twenty.' She burst out laughing. 'I've had plenty of sex since then and everything that goes with it too. You know what I mean. The dramatic bits – the rows, the tenderness, the excitement. But I'm not desperate to do it all the time any more.'

They talked together for hours.

Suddenly Katarina found herself confiding about Jack. About when he had hit her.

Ulla sighed. 'I knew you grew up with a violent father. Olof told me that. I think girls with that in their background are often attracted to violent men later on. My advice, Katarina, is lose that guy fast, for Christ's sake.'

The clock struck four. Ulla had to hurry off to collect her boys after school.

34

On the following Saturday afternoon, Ingrid and Viktor Emmanuel stepped out of their taxi on shaky legs. They were fed cheese omelette in the Elgs' kitchen then went home to sleep.

Katarina checked her hospital bag: baby clothes, sponge-bag, a nightdress, a dressing-gown. Not that she hadn't checked it often enough before – but you never know, she thought.

It was raining. Ingrid, awake again after a few hours' sleep, thought this was a blessing. It had been too dry recently.

It rained all weekend. On Monday morning, Viktor Emmanuel came for coffee in Katarina's kitchen. 'I'll take you two to the health centre in my car,' he said. 'It's bigger than yours and, anyway, it'll save you driving.'

'Thank you.'

Dr Gille looked tired and worn, like most family doctors. He asked Katarina questions while he listened to Elisabeth's heart. Then he said he wanted a blood sample and wrote a referral note for an ECG.

Katarina, who had been calm, felt a tight knot of anxiety forming inside her. They were shown into a little waiting room and sat there for what seemed like an eternity. Katarina clung to Viktor's hand, which was clammy with sweat. He's afraid too, she thought.

Finally the doctor came to talk to them. He explained that Elisabeth's coronary arteries were almost blocked. 'Mrs Elg should be seen immediately by a cardiologist. I've phoned Karolinska Hospital in Stockholm and they're getting a bed ready for her. Nurse is organizing an ambulance. In my view an operation is probably unavoidable, but first Mrs Elg must be thoroughly examined.'

'May we travel with her in the ambulance?'

'Of course. You mustn't burden her with your anxiety, though.'

He shook Katarina's hand and said he sympathized with her. Her husband must be such a support to her.

It was the first time the artist had been mistaken for her husband . . . but there's always a first time.

They were awed by the efficiency of the staff at the vast hospital. In a matter of minutes Elisabeth was in bed with a drip in place. Electrodes were taped to her chest so that a machine could record her heartbeats.

Afterwards they were left to sit for interminable hours in another waiting room. Finally two doctors arrived: one was older and compassionate, the other young and energetic.

'Mrs Elg's operation will be scheduled relatively soon, within the next couple of weeks. Meanwhile we'll keep her here under observation. We want to do some investigations. The evidence suggests that she might have been close to an infarction.' The young man's voice was cold, with a hint of reproach. Then he nodded and left.

The older doctor said, 'We'll try a PTCA; Percutaneous Transluminal Coronary Angioplasty.'

Katarina did not understand the incomprehensible medical terminology. Viktor Emmanuel did, though. He had friends who had undergone a similar operation.

'It's miraculous,' he said, when they settled down to sandwiches and coffee in the hospital cafeteria. 'I'll tell you what they do.' And he explained how a tube would be inserted though a big artery in Elisabeth's groin and pushed up into the heart's own network of arteries. Then a miniature camera and several balloons would be sent up the tube. The balloons would be inflated and – bang! – the blockage area would be cleared.

'It sounds unbelievable.'

'It does, doesn't it? One thing's for sure, they rarely fail. Elisabeth should be back home in a few weeks' time.'

At that Katarina fell silent.

He left her then to phone Olof.

'What did Olof say?'

'That the whole family now has gastric flu, every one of them. I told him not to come anywhere near this place – no fucking viruses in the surgical wards, please. Come on, let's take a taxi back to the car. Bet you I'll have a bloody parking ticket.'

He won his bet.

Ingrid had been round and had tidied up. She had just made the beds with clean sheets when they arrived. Katarina fell asleep at once.

Then Olof phoned. He wanted to speak to Viktor Emmanuel, but Ingrid told him Viktor was out.

'Where is he?' Olof snapped.

'Calm down. He's gone into town to argue with the police. I'll tell him to call you as soon as he's back.'

Viktor called Olof. 'Katarina is sleeping like a baby. There's been no message from the Karolinska and that means nothing has happened. I'll be sleeping on Katarina's sitting-room sofa tonight. I promise not to let her out of my sight for a moment.'

'Why were you arguing with the police?'

'A small matter of a parking ticket. They saw the light and tore it up.' Viktor laughed uproariously.

Olof said that he, too, was in for a hospital visit. Apparently he had the wrong kind of bacteria in his stomach.

'Or gut or whatever,' Viktor Emmanuel said. 'Sounds delightful. Anyway, we'll keep you informed.'

When Katarina woke she wanted something soothing to eat. A bowl of tapioca. There was no argument, and she got what she wanted. Then she went to the bathroom and straight back to bed.

Viktor Emmanuel bedded down on the sofa, muttering about

how narrow it was. He soon fell asleep. The desk lamp spread a soft light in the room.

When the artist sleeps he doesn't snore, he hums, Katarina thought. She liked the sound he made and soon slept too.

Viktor woke at Katarina's cry. He glanced at the clock. It was almost two a.m. He hurried into her bedroom and found her sitting up in bed, her eyes huge and terrified. 'I dreamt I was swimming! I woke and there was water everywhere.' It was dripping from her bed.

Viktor snatched up the phone and made a call. 'Right. Ten minutes, no longer,' he said.

'Don't worry,' said the voice at the other end. 'It's usual for it to start with the waters breaking. The baby has kicked a hole in the membranes surrounding it.'

He helped her take off her nightdress, then found a clean one and folded a towel to put between her legs. Finally, he put her dressing-gown round her shoulders.

'The baby couldn't take yesterday's scares,' she said.

He didn't reply because the ambulance had arrived. Katarina was carried down on a stretcher. She held on to her hospital bag and her jaws were clenched.

'Are you in pain?' the paramedic asked.

'Not really. It's just an ache, stronger at times.'

'Relax. Your husband's there for you, holding your hand.'

Before he got into the ambulance with Katarina, Viktor remembered to push his keys through Ingrid's letter-box. He forgot to pick up his wallet, though.

The maternity ward was calm. A midwife came, listened to the foetal heartbeat, checked Katarina's cervix and announced that the baby was keen to get on with it.

'Is everything normal?'

'So, you're the father. Well, you'll want to be at the birth, won't you?'

'Sure,' Viktor said. He was given a clean white coat and told to wash his hands. From the labour suite, he heard Katarina cry out. He became rigid with fear, wanted to run, wanted to say that he couldn't bear it . . . She screamed again. He recognized the sound from childhood. Pigs screamed like that when they were slaughtered.

The midwife saw him pale. 'Now, we've no time for fainting fathers here. Sit down there, by her head. Help her to breathe nice and slow. And to push when the time comes.'

She attached Katarina to a machine and wandered off. Other women were giving birth that night. He could hear them screaming.

Minutes became hours. The contractions came and went. He wanted to escape. Between escape plans, he realised he'd never understood quite what women had to . . . all their peculiarities seemed acceptable, now that he'd seen this . . .

Then, another contraction. He said, 'Push as hard as you can.' Another contraction. Then another. It was close to five o'clock in the morning. Katarina screamed that she was bursting.

Then the midwife materialized from somewhere. 'Here she comes! Head first, just as she should.'

Five minutes later, something like a large fish slipped out of Katarina's belly. The midwife checked the baby girl and laid her on her mother's belly.

'Hearing the beating of each other's heart,' she explained vaguely. Viktor Emmanuel could not see the point. The thing on Katarina's body looked like a frog, but grey and smeared with fat.

He was sent to the cafeteria. Meanwhile, Katarina would be washed and stitched. Then they would wash the baby and snip it.

'Snip?'

'Oh, the umbilical cord.'

'Silly me.'

It was when he tried to pay for the coffee that he realized he had left his wallet at home. He had his mobile, thank God. He dialled Uppsala and Olof came to the phone. Viktor Emmanuel reported the night's events briefly. Olof had been declared virus-free and would come immediately, he said.

'OK, that means I can order bacon and eggs. You see, I've got no money.'

35

Viktor Emmanuel was sitting in the far corner of the cafeteria. He looked more dishevelled than ever. His eyes were bloodshot and half closed.

He managed to smile when he saw Olof. 'Brilliant. You've come.'

He had not finished the fried eggs. The yolks were staring at them from the greasy plate like yellow eyeballs.

Olof fetched himself a cup of coffee. He joined Viktor and they sat together in silence.

Then Viktor Emmanuel spoke. 'Tonight I've finally got some insight into why women are . . . women. Stubborn, mad when they're in love, as flexible as rubber-bands but rock solid at the same time.'

'Strong stuff. Katarina would be furious if she heard you.'

Viktor wasn't listening. 'What hell they have to go through. Somehow, we owe them everything.'

Olof nodded.

Viktor's face was rigid. 'I was sure she'd die,' he said, through clenched teeth. 'I thought no one could survive such pain.' He fell silent. 'Ever been around when pigs are slaughtered?'

'I grew up in the countryside.'

'She screamed like a stuck pig.' Another long silence. 'After four hours of pain a frog-like creature popped out. They put it on her stomach. Then they got shot of me, saying they were going to stitch a split bit together, that everything was fine, and the frog was a sweet little girl.'

Olof phoned Katarina's ward and learnt that mother and baby were doing well, he was welcome to visit at midday, and must bring the father. If the poor man had survived the delivery, of course.

'He survived, but only just,' Olof said.

The nurse at the end of the phone burst out laughing.

It was eight o'clock in the morning. Somehow, Olof thought, he must find a place for Viktor to sleep. He had found the artist sagging like an empty sack on the uncomfortable cafeteria chair. 'Come on, we're going for a trip in the car.'

Viktor rose and followed him, zombie-like, to the car park. Olof pulled down the back seat in his large Volvo, inflated a rubber mattress and shook out a couple of blankets.

'Here, you crawl in and go to sleep. I'll drive slowly round Djurgården Park, which will be very quiet just now. The hum of the engine will put you to sleep. OK?'

'Come off it.'

'Try me.'

Viktor was asleep before Olof had left the car park.

The big car crept past tidy front gardens, beside huge golf courses, then past villas that practically smelt of tradition and money. The May sun shone over the fresh green of new leaves and grass and deep blue sea inlets.

How pretty it all was.

He drove north along the promenade until the buildings gave way to open countryside. Then a huge edifice, a gigantic oval shape, rose in front of him. A hangar. He was at the abandoned military aerodrome at Hägernäs. Good, no human presence anywhere, no voices except the birds' singing in the big trees along the beach. He stopped a few metres from the water, switched off the engine and breathed in deeply. On the other side of the bay, trees climbed a low ridge.

After a few minutes Viktor Emmanuel stirred in the back of the car. Then he sat up, looked around and saw the hangar. His eyes widened. 'What a fantastic place. Great proportions, good lines. What is it?'

'An abandoned hangar. An air squadron was once stationed here. Sea planes, ready to defend Sweden to the last.'

They walked together into the bushes and had a pee, side by side.

'Were you called up?'

'I was. Air force actually, in Halmstad.'

'I was in Boden.'

'Sounds bloody cold.'

'You're so right.'

Walking back to the car, Olof said, 'You look awful. I've got a shaving-kit, soap and a toothbrush in the car.'

Viktor Emmanuel took the sponge-bag down to the water's edge and washed, combed his hair and shaved and trimmed his beard, as well as he could.

When they returned to the car, the terrors of the night were reflected in his eyes. 'Katarina is alone – we must . . . She's in pain and we've abandoned her.'

'She's fine,' Olof said, and told Viktor about his phone call to the ward.

'Professional liars every one of them . . .'

'Viktor, calm down. They're not lying and they really are professionals in the baby business. Deliveries all night every night. If they say it went normally, then it did.'

They both laughed.

After a while Olof found the courage to ask, 'What's between you and Katarina?'

Viktor Emmanuel smiled. 'She proposed to me, you know.'

'I'm not surprised. That's just what my sister would do. So, if I may ask, what was your answer?'

'I asked for some time to think about it.'

'Why?'

'Because I want to see that American. Well, see the two of them together.'

'So, she hasn't told you . . .'

'Told me what?'

Olof struck the steering-wheel with his fist, and his voice was very deep when he told Viktor to listen to him.

He began by explaining Katarina's visit to their mother's cottage by the river Ljusnan and how, when they had parted, Elisabeth had gone back to Gävle while Katarina returned to Stockholm. Katarina had promised to phone Elisabeth as soon as she got back to her flat. 'So when she had not phoned by two o'clock in the morning, Elisabeth was worried. It wasn't like Katarina not to phone. Elisabeth got in touch with me. I had keys to Katarina's flat in Stockholm and I drove there at once. I found her lying on the floor, barely conscious. There was blood everywhere. I called for an ambulance and waited all night at the hospital while they operated on her. I passed the time working out ways and means to murder the American.' Olof groaned. He hit the steering-wheel again. 'Her left ear was fucked up. She still hasn't got normal hearing back. Haven't you noticed how she turns her head to the right when you talk to her?'

'I don't want to hear this. Let me get out,' Viktor shouted. Olof stopped the car and he stumbled out, jogged round the car, came back and groaned. 'Then what happened?' he asked.

'We took her in to look after her. She was poorly for weeks. Erika helped her a lot. The doctors wanted her to press charges against the American, but she refused. Anyway, he had left Sweden.'

Viktor Emmanuel got back into the car. 'Why doesn't she talk about it?'

'Erika believes that Katarina feels ashamed. That sounds odd, but apparently it's common in violated women.'

Now Olof got out of the car, took some deep breaths and tried to relax his hands. After a while he went on, 'The physical injuries were not the worst part of it, Viktor. The violence brought back old traumas from long ago. You see, our father abused our mother for years. Katarina, who was barely five when it started, had to tend Mama's injuries.'

Viktor Emmanuel stared at Olof blankly and shook his head. 'That can't be true. Not Elisabeth?'

'It's true, Viktor.'

It was getting near midday. Time to go back to the hospital.

'I need a drink or three.'

'Me too, but . . .'

'I know.'

'We should have brought some flowers,' Olof said. But the room was already glowing with flowers, brought by Ingrid and Ulla.

And Katarina was sitting up in bed with a tiny bundle at her breast. 'You're beaming like the midnight sun,' Olof said, and everyone laughed.

They began to discuss the future.

Elisabeth was under constant observation and complained that she had been immobilized. She had had a heart X-ray, which had been uncomfortable but not painful. She must not get excited under any circumstance.

Erika had told Katarina all this in a long telephone call. She was at the Karolinska, waiting to see Elisabeth's medical team.

'I'll call her mobile,' Olof said. He listened without saying much, and arranged to collect Erika within the hour. 'Good news,' he told them. 'They think the operation will work and they're going to do it in a week or so.'

Erika had asked them if she could tell Elisabeth that her new grandchild had been born, but the doctor had advised against it. She might excite herself, he said.

Katarina suggested that Elisabeth would be more likely to get upset if she heard nothing and they looked uncertainly at each other.

Then Olof confessed that he had told Viktor Emmanuel about what Jack had done.

'Good,' Katarina said.

She turned to the artist. 'You must forgive me for not telling you myself. Just thinking about it made me feel sick at heart. Look on the bottom shelf of my bedside table at home. You'll find a bundle of letters from Mama to me. Please read them when you can – you must be so tired now.'

Before they left, she said, 'Mama told me of a strange experience she had when she was almost comatose once. She said she felt as though she was wandering around inside her own soul and that everything there seemed so light and clear. That's where I am now, even though I'm fully conscious.'

36

Erika, at Karolinska Hospital, suddenly made up her mind. She tiptoed into Elisabeth's room, held her hand and whispered, 'Katarina's baby has been born and the delivery went normally. The baby is healthy and perfectly lovely and Katarina is beaming like the sun, Olof says.'

The relieved smile on Elisabeth's face showed that she had heard and understood.

Then Erika told her, 'Katarina was not alone for a second. Viktor Emmanuel was with her all night. Olof says he's quite shaken by it all.'

Elisabeth's smile grew broader.

Then the nurse came hurrying along and told Erika not to worry Mrs Elg. The monitor had shown a blip.

Erika took the nurse aside and told her what had happened. The good news would calm the patient and her heart. Elisabeth had been anxious about her daughter giving birth to her first child. The nurse nodded and said, 'I'm sure you did the right thing, but let's not mention it to anyone else.'

'I'll be back as soon as I can.'

'Fine.'

'Could you let me have five minutes more just now?'

'Yes, of course, but no more excitements.'

'I promise.'

The nurse went back to watching her monitors and noted with surprise that Mrs Elg's heart was pumping normally.

Erika was sitting close to the bed, moving her hands over Elisabeth's body, from her feet to the top of her head, lingering over her heart.

Elisabeth fell asleep. 'Soon you'll be well and back at home,' Erika whispered.

Later, Olof came to collect her. He had lent Viktor Emmanuel some money and helped him to find a taxi.

At home at Oxel Street, the artist found Katarina's house tidy and clean and a hot meal waiting for him. After a huge brandy, he fell into bed and heard Ingrid say that it was amazing how much water she'd had in her belly, poor girl.

After ten hours' sleep in Katarina's bed, and an hour soaking in her bath, he decided he was no longer sure whose house he was in. It was a pleasant thought.

Carefully, he tried to examine his memories of the night before. The screaming, the unbearable, inhuman screaming.

He went back to his studio and tried to fix the images from the birth on paper and canvas. He failed, but was not upset. His feelings were still too raw. The intensity had to fade and mature.

Suddenly an image of a canyon, stratified stone exposed on sheer rock-faces, countless colours in layer upon layer of ancient minerals and then, deep down, roaring river water . . . Something in this sketch looked right and he left it pinned to the easel.

He looked into Elisabeth's garden. The rockery was covered with violets in full bloom. Thousands of tiny flowers looked at him with golden eyes from within shining blue and deep violet petals.

Then Ingrid arrived with her camera. 'Who could have guessed that all this would be in the soil that came with the stones?'

He picked a huge bouquet and took it to Katarina that afternoon. She was just as happy as she had been earlier and laughed when he gave her the violets. 'Another miracle of growth!'

Her only problem was that she had too much milk. 'I feel like a cow with leaking udders. They've got to milk me before I can start feeding the baby. She's not very good at sucking but that's normal in the beginning, they say.

'I think I've decided on the names – all of them,' she said.

'Tell me.'

'Laila, after Erika's white-witch grandmother. Who knows?

The name may be magic and the baby turn out to have special powers.'

Viktor nodded.

'She must be called Elisabeth after Mama, of course. Then I thought of Viktoria. After you. Don't you think Laila Elisabeth Viktoria sounds impressive?'

He did not say anything but Katarina saw the delight on his face.

'There is another small problem. They're short of beds and want to send me home tomorrow.'

This worried him. 'Now, for Christ's sake . . .'

'I called Nurse Birgitta at the clinic. She'll come and help. And I've phoned Erika. She'll leave the boys with Ulla and come out to give you some time off on Friday.'

'I don't need time off,' Viktor said.

'Neither of us will get much sleep, you know. Brand-new babies don't take much notice of whether it's day or night.'

When Viktor Emmanuel had gone, Katarina reflected that he had not taken any interest in the baby, which was a pity. Still, he'd get used to her, in time.

The artist was astounded by the amount of kit that a tiny new person needed. Scales to be weighed on, a basin to be bathed in, a table to be changed on, bottles and sterilizing equipment for extra milk, and a mountain of bedlinen and nappies. Ingrid brought a little cradle, which she put next to Katarina's bed. She did not mention where she had found it. Then Viktor remembered an old rocking-chair in his attic and felt it might come in handy.

When everything was ready he made some coffee and offered Nurse Birgitta a cup. He told her how appalled he had been by the horrors of childbirth. 'I fully believed that Katarina would die, her pain seemed unbearable.'

'Hasn't it occurred to you that the baby had the hardest time of you all? Imagine being surrounded by warm water, peaceful and calm, then suddenly being made to fight your way, inch by inch, through a narrow tunnel – only to emerge into a ghastly, cold world full of loud noises, screaming, hard metal. And, adding insult to injury, having to breathe air.'

Viktor Emmanuel was silenced. Birgitta continued, 'I believe that being born is our first encounter with fear and that afterwards fear stays with us throughout life.'

Next day, when they left the hospital, Viktor Emmanuel offered to carry little Laila. Katarina heard him whisper, 'You're a bloody brave baby.'

June began and with it the baby's life at home. No one who had heard him would ever forget Viktor Emmanuel's singing during the bright nights of summer. Up and down he walked, the baby in his arms. 'The Owl and the Pussycat went to sea . . .'

37

A letter with American stamps arrived, addressed to Katarina. At first she did not want to open it, but then she saw that it had come from 'Janet Morris Legal Practice.'

That made her curious.

Dear Katarina,

I must begin by trying to explain who I am and my connection with the O'Hara family. The latter in particular is problematic, both to explain and to understand. I'm Ed O'Hara's partner and thus Jack's sort-of stepmother. However, I had never met Jack until he turned up in my New York home last autumn. He was a wreck then, beaten up and hung over.

I am black and grew up in Harlem. I was the fifth child of a worn-out mother. Now, my siblings are all dead. I never knew why my mother's church decided to invest in my education, but I went to college and then to university, where I studied law.

My background makes it easy to understand why I devoted much of my time to assisting abused women. My main aim is to get them divorce on reasonable conditions. In the United States, this is far from straightforward and in the beginning I often lost my cases. Gradually, I learnt more about one aspect, which is the hopeless inability of my women clients to act effectively on their own behalf.

I wrote a book on the subject, which to my amazement started a wide-ranging debate on domestic violence. During that time, I received a letter attempting to analyse why some men become abusive and violent. It was written by a businessman called Ed O'Hara.

I was not impressed by his arguments. I felt that I had already written clearly enough about how little boys who are beaten become violent men. But I agreed to meet him and it was an interesting encounter because it opened my eyes to the role of mothers in these gruesome domestic games.

You may find all this boring, so I shall end this account quickly. I soon became very fond of Ed, and later, more than fond. I feel a similar, deep empathy with Jack, who might have been too damaged at an early stage for him ever to become a whole human being.

On behalf of the two O'Haras and myself I am delighted to accept the invitation to the christening in Stockholm on 15 June. You may be interested to know that I am a gospel singer and said to be a good one. Please consult with your brother, who presumably will officiate, about the possibility of my singing something at the end of the ceremony.

With my warmest good wishes,

Janet

While the baby slept that afternoon, Katarina wrote an answer to the letter.

Dear Janet,

I am so grateful for your letter, which meant a lot to me. Naturally, I have wondered about you and the way you were able to sort out the problems and get us talking. Before, the families were too divided.

My baby has arrived and she is the loveliest creature. I had no idea such happiness was possible.

I am grateful for what you tell me about Jack. I had already arrived at a decision about our relationship. He and I have nothing in common, we come from different cultures and have different values. During one lovely summer, we enjoyed each other's bodies but that is something I feel we will never experience again. I am afraid of him and always will be. This is not just because he injured me physically. My fears go back to my childhood, because my father often hit my mother when I was still a little girl. During most of my life, I have found it hard to forgive her for putting up with this. She was a teacher and could have earned enough to support her two children.

When Jack hit me, these terrible memories came back. I was plagued with thoughts about the inheritance of behaviour patterns.

My mother has been ill recently with a serious heart condition but has had an operation that has cured her. Incredible what the doctors can do. She is back home now, running up and down the stairs and spending hours chattering with her granddaughter.

I spoke to Olof about you singing at the christening. He thought it was a lovely idea. He would like you to fax your music to his organist and will send you the address, phone and fax numbers. Olof asked me to mention that the church has a very high roof.

We look forward to having you with us here. My best wishes,

Katarina

Fax from J.G. Habner, Organist (Uppsala) to Janet Morris (New York)
Thanks for the music you sent. Your song is not quite 'big' enough for the church and not at all known over here. May I suggest a Swedish song that is often sung in American churches? You are sure to recognize it, because it hit the charts some years ago when Elvis Presley sang a version of it. The melody comes from a Swedish folk-song and the lyrics were written by a Swedish pastor, a long time ago – actually a hundred years ago or more. Try it, think about it.

Fax from Janet Morris to J.G. Habner
It's a wonderful song. I know it well. Let's do it!

Email from Olof Elg to Janet Morris
The organist has asked me to find out if you could come a couple of days early for rehearsals. If there's a convenient flight on Thursday, I'll meet you at the airport and look after you.

Olof

Email to Olof Elg from Janet Morris

We have to travel via Frankfurt because Ed has to attend an important business meeting there. The plane from Frankfurt arrives in Stockholm at three on Thursday afternoon. We will do the rehearsals on Friday while Jack shows his father around Stockholm. We are booked in at the Grand Hotel.

Janet

38

June was lovely, a month generous with golden days and pale blue nights.

'Never fear, it will start raining in time for the christening,' muttered Ingrid, who kept moving the sprinkler. The dry weather drove her to swear aloud.

Olof picked up his mother from the hospital two days after her operation. She has changed, he thought. She is quieter, less quick to argue, but happier than he had seen her for a long time. Both she and Katarina had wept when they met.

Elisabeth spent the morning sitting by the baby's cradle. No one knew what took place between the two, but when the baby woke she smiled at her grandmother.

It was her first smile. Ingrid said it was probably wind, but when Katarina came in to feed her, the miracle happened once more.

When Viktor Emmanuel turned up that afternoon to hum a little song at her bedside, she smiled at him too, unmistakably. 'She's becoming human,' he said.

Olof asked Viktor Emmanuel if they could have a private talk. Viktor, surprised at his serious tone, agreed at once. They went across to his studio.

'I've had an idea,' Olof said. 'I want to reinstate the roles of godfather and godmother. You know the old custom: a godparent used to take some responsibility for a child.'

'Wasn't that mostly a financial commitment? Just in case something happened. Nowadays, of course, it's rare for parents to die young.'

'On the other hand, many parents divorce, and ordinary families are often in straitened circumstances. They lack both time and money for the children. Relatives can be far away.'

'And if they live nearby they're often short of time too,' Viktor agreed.

Olof nodded. 'Then there is what I suppose we could call the spirit of the times – confusion about norms, different values, pressures generated by the media, endless images of violence and cruelty.' He thought for a while and continued, 'People seem to agree that children need more adults around them, at school and in nurseries. Mature people, who have a genuine interest in children and are able to offer support and continuity.'

Viktor Emmanuel stared at Olof. 'What a dreamer you are. But, then, so am I. Count me in. Do godparents sign a contract of some kind?'

'No, but at the christening they are asked to state their commitment to the baby.'

'A sacred promise?'

'With any luck,' Olof said, and sighed.

'So, your idea is that I should become a godfather?'

'Well, no. Not now. It seemed obvious at first but later . . .'

'What?'

'Later it seemed even more obvious that you're going to be the baby's father. Or am I wrong?'

'Not bloody likely. Of course I'll be taking care of Laila.'

They were silent for a time.

'Whom do you have in mind now?'

'Ingrid and Lars – he's our plumber but a friend too. They will take it seriously and they are responsible people who love children. Then there's Jack O'Hara. I'm afraid I've promised him this already.'

'It doesn't bother me.' But Viktor was a poor liar.

Before they parted, Viktor said, 'I'll be in church for the ceremony, of course, but afterwards I'm going straight to Borlänge.' He laughed. 'Don't look so surprised. I must tell my mother, that's all.'

The sun had sunk behind the hills but a golden light still

illuminated the world. Elisabeth was sitting in her garden and admiring the violets covering her rockery. Ingrid brought her a jug of home-made currant drink, found a chair and sat down. She nodded in agreement when Elisabeth mused, 'Some things are miraculous.'

They were thinking of Katarina and Viktor Emmanuel.

Then Ingrid said, looking at the violets, 'There was a pile of quite sandy soil next to where we picked up the stones. It was almost certainly acidic, but if the ferns, fuchsias and all the other flowers you wanted are to do well, we need to bed them in rich topsoil. And use plenty of lime to make it alkaline enough. The violets will hate it.'

'That's such a pity.'

'But they'll soon be over now. Surely you'd like something else on your rockery?'

'Of course I would – it's just that there's something magic about violets. As if they know what we're longing for and try to comfort us.' Elisabeth pointed to a small vase on the table in front of them. They contemplated the little flowers and Ingrid nodded again.

They were interrupted when Katarina arrived with Laila at her breast. The baby sucked a little more, then fell asleep in the sunshine, content.

Soon Olof and Viktor joined them and told them what they had been talking about. Elisabeth said she understood why Viktor wanted to see his mother. Katarina smiled a little wryly and said that if he had decided to be Laila's daddy he couldn't be her godfather.

Olof's forehead creased. He knew that smile of his sister's well enough and it occurred to him that perhaps Viktor Emmanuel had over-simplified the situation.

Ingrid looked at Katarina: her eyes held a warning.

Later that evening, when the women were all in the kitchen together, Ingrid said, 'If you marry Viktor Emmanuel you'll spend your life on an emotional roller-coaster. I'm not saying he isn't trustworthy, just that in some ways he's like a child. He's always curious, which is the basis for his work. He'll chase after new challenges whenever they turn up – and I don't just mean women. Any new experience might make him restless.'

' "Quoth the raven . . ." Ingrid, you're such a pessimist.' Elisabeth sounded cross.

Katarina laughed. 'Ingrid, I think you think I'm a bit of a fool. I'm not, you know. Viktor Emmanuel is rather like the Owl, or maybe the Pussycat, off to sea . . .'

Elisabeth stared at her, wide-eyed. Katarina had to explain about the baby's first nights at home and Viktor singing to her through the night. ' "The Owl and the Pussycat" seemed to suit him so well . . .'

Katarina sang a verse for them.

> 'The Owl and the Pussy-Cat went to sea
> In a beautiful pea-green boat:
> They took some honey and plenty of money
> Wrapped up in a five-pound note.
> The Owl looked up to the stars above,
> And sang to a small guitar,
> "O lovely Pussy, O Pussy, my love,
> What a beautiful Pussy you are,
> You are, You are!
> What a beautiful Pussy you are!" '

'No mother turned up to try to stop *them* getting married,' Ingrid said and laughed.

'True enough. They just danced in the light of the moon,' Katarina said.

39

Summer held Sweden in a firm grip. There were warnings of forest fires on radio and television, farmers complained and gardeners watered their plots endlessly. Towards nine in the evening the sun tried to sink below the north-western horizon, but it never quite managed it.

The glowing evening light filled the arrivals hall, where Olof was waiting for the plane from Frankfurt.

Then he saw them: first a slim, elegant woman with dark skin. She moved with a dancer's grace, eagerly observing everything. Her mobile face broke into a broad smile. After her, as a discreet escort, came two tall men.

Olof, in jeans with his crumpled linen jacket thrown over one shoulder, straightened and went to meet them. 'You must be Janet Morris. I am Olof Elg. I'm so pleased to meet you.'

'You can't be Olof Elg!'

'Well, I am. Why not?'

'I know what a pastor should look like – probably a beard, definitely over fifty with the kind of piercing eyes that can see every sin hidden at the back of your soul. You're too young and too good-looking. Incredible!'

'American pastors must be an ugly bunch.'

'You said it,' Jack said, and smiled. Then he added, 'Olof looks like his sister. He's got to be who he says he is.'

They all laughed and shook hands. A wave of resentment washed over Olof when he was faced with Jack, but he liked the father.

When they were all packed into the Volvo, with the luggage, Janet said, 'I'd love to see the cathedral where the christening is going to take place.'

'I'm sorry, it's to the north of here and we're driving south, to Stockholm,' Olof told her.

'But it's so light. Night seems far away.'

'A couple of months, actually,' Olof said. 'So, OK. Let's go.'

He phoned the warden of Uppsala Cathedral, who promised to open it for the visitors.

'I'll be interested to know how you've imagined it. It's very old and respectable, unlike me.'

Olof had been joking, but Janet sounded serious when she started to describe her idea of a Swedish church: at the edge of a deep forest, simply furnished with pews hewn from pine logs, a plain altar covered by a white cloth, a small hand organ.

'You'll get the surprise of your life,' Olof said.

The cathedral astounded them, especially Janet, who covered her eyes with her hands and had to wait a little before looking at it again. 'I've got to sit down,' she said. 'Wow, I must take this in slowly, a little at a time.'

Olof led the two men along, told them briefly about the kings and nobles whose tombs stood in the side chapels. Jack and Ed stopped spontaneously in front of the magnificent chapel where King Gustav Vasa and his two queens were enthroned against a background of blue and gold.

Then Olof returned to Janet, who was sitting at the far end of the aisle where she could see the line of huge Gothic arches.

'Does God take pleasure in His house?'

'I don't know, but I have felt His presence here, under this roof.'

'I expect you have,' she said easily, but her eyes were almost frightened. 'And my small voice, what will it sound like here?'

'You know best. Remember, I told you it had a high roof.'

'High roof!'

They laughed.

As they left the cathedral, Ed said, 'If you planned to impress us, you succeeded, Olof.'

'That's good,' Olof replied. He was on the phone, trying to book a taxi.

As they got the luggage out of the car, Jack said, 'I've heard a great deal about your Sami population, but I guess they're living pretty far up north?'

'If you want to speak to a Sami, why don't you try my wife Erika? She knows a lot of Sami people – many are her relatives, of course.'

When they were in the taxi going south on the E4, Jack said, 'That handsome young priest is married to a Sami woman and has two Chinese children. What do you make of that?' He sounded baffled.

'No more mysteries,' Janet mumbled. She had almost fallen asleep in the car. All three of them needed to rest. Huge soft beds were waiting for them at the Grand Hotel.

Early the next morning, Jack arranged to hire a car. They had breakfast together, looking out over the lakeside city.

'What's that large, square building?'

'The Swedish king's castle.'

At the stroke of ten that morning Janet was waiting at the great door of Uppsala Cathedral. The young organist came to meet her. Thank God, he seems perfectly ordinary – nothing exotic here, Janet thought. 'I had a fright yesterday when I saw how large the cathedral is,' she said to the organist. 'I don't think my voice will fill this vast space.'

'You'll be fine,' he said. 'Just remember to wait for the echo.'

They started to rehearse.

40

The christening day had arrived. The Americans were at the cathedral in good time and a small, square-built young woman came to meet them. She introduced herself as Erika, Olof's wife. Plain-looking girl, Janet thought, as they shook hands. She herself was resplendent in white silk taffeta while Erika wore a white cotton blouse and a grey skirt.

'I've been asked to be your interpreter and guide,' Erika said. 'There's some time before the service starts, so you might be interested in looking round the chapel to your right.'

It was a gloomy place, with one large sarcophagus. Janet, who felt a little tense, sat down on the base and leant back against its side. The young woman laughed and, somehow, her solidity vanished.

Why, she's so pretty, Ed thought.

'Janet, have you ever heard of Swedenborg?' Erika asked.

'Yes, he was into a kind of spiritualism, wasn't he? And founded a church on the basis of it. One of my uncles was a member.'

'You're sitting on his coffin.'

Janet leapt up and clapped her hand over her mouth to suppress a shriek.

'Don't worry, he likes you – I'm sure he doesn't mind.'

Janet sat down again.

'And how do you know he likes Janet?' Jack asked, in a jocular tone.

'I couldn't tell you exactly and, anyway, I don't want to know how I know these things,' Erika replied seriously.

She noticed their surprise at her answer and looked amused. 'In life and death, Swedenborg was a remarkable man,' she continued. 'What happened after his death was strange. His remains were brought here and buried with a lot of ceremony. It was somewhat embarrassing that his head was missing.'

Her listeners' eyes were focused on her. She laughed. 'A few years ago, it became known that Swedenborg's head was going to be sold at an auction in London. I'm not sure what the story was but some Swedes bid for it and brought it home. Then the sarcophagus here was opened and the head buried with the rest.' She giggled. 'I've often thought that the spirit of Swedenborg was watching from up there somewhere, surrounded by angels, and laughing at the whole performance.'

Jack looked bewildered. 'That sounds like a tall tale.'

'I suppose it does,' Erika admitted, still smiling. 'Still, there's plenty of documentation to prove it.'

'What's the view of Swedish scientists about Swedenborg's spiritual world?' Ed asked.

'Oh, Ed, you know what scientists say nowadays. The last I heard was that someone had decided Swedenborg was a poet, which meant his spiritual writings were reduced to . . . literature, something like a fantasy novel.'

She looked at the clock and said that they had to move on. 'The other guests must have a chance to meet you before the christening.'

In the aisle, Elisabeth was waiting to greet them. She had the poise of an upper-class Englishwoman, Janet thought. She was polite if distant with Jack, but when she shook hands with Ed, her greeting was warm. Then she turned to Janet and tears stood in her eyes. 'I'd like to give you a hug,' she said, and they fell into each other's arms.

Ed met the plumber and his plump little wife, then the brusque Ingrid Kristiansson, and a thickset, shabby-looking character who called himself Karlsson. After him there was another guy, then a whole row of academics, mostly women. By now all the Swedish names were becoming unmanageable.

Everybody seemed friendly enough, but the smiles became a little strained as Erika struggled with the introductions.

'Where is Katarina?' Jack had tried to whisper it to Elisabeth but it echoed back at him.

'She's in one of the side chapels, feeding the baby.'

Jack had a vision of Katarina's lovely breasts. He felt repelled at the idea of milk coming out of them. At least Grace had had the good taste not to breastfeed.

The organist played a solemn march, and the group walked slowly towards the altar where the christening would take place.

'It's an historic building, with connections to many of the Swedish kings,' Erika whispered. 'And you mustn't miss the windows.'

They looked up. Janet almost whistled with delight.

They were shown into their seats, arranged in two rows facing each other. Elisabeth held a little boy on her lap and another sat next to her. Both waved to Erika.

It's true, Janet thought, they are Chinese.

Then Katarina arrived with the baby in her arms. She sat down at her mother's side.

She was wearing a long white dress and her thick blonde hair was pulled up into a crown on top of her head. The arrangement showed off her clean profile and long neck. She was poised, gracious.

Jack was transfixed. She looked even more beautiful than he remembered.

Katarina nodded to the American guests and, seeing Ed, thought how alike they were, father and son. The same friendly but reserved, sardonic smile and the same grey eyes. Maybe Ed's eyes were more serious and steady than Jack's. She smiled at Janet, with a hint of complicity.

Finally, Jack. She had prepared herself for seeing him again but her reaction still took her by surprise. A wave of regret and wild longing swept through her. It was as if her feelings had remained the same during the year they had been apart, even though it had been a momentous period of change and rebirth.

The baby sensed her agitation and woke with a little squeak of displeasure. Katarina was grateful for the diversion. Now she could lift the baby, put her tiny face beside her own and hope that no one had noticed her blush.

Still, the confusion stayed with her throughout the ceremony and she could not take in Olof's sermon or the promises made by the godparents. Later she felt disappointed with herself.

The thunderous notes of the organ softened into a simple hymn tune. The Swedish congregation sang the familiar words about God's gift of summer. The Americans were amazed that everyone seemed to know them by heart.

The pastor stood at the altar and led the congregation in praying: 'Our Father, Who art in heaven . . .' Janet felt she recognized every word, in spite of the foreign language. The same prayer we say in my church – and the same faith, she thought.

Olof spoke about the child: how she had arrived among them as a joyous gift. How they must care for her with love and commitment.

Erika translated in whispers for Janet, who nodded now and then, touched and absorbed.

He went on to talk about the godparents: they had been chosen with great care and their role demanded responsibility and engagement. 'In the society we live in today, the family – especially a small family – is under constant pressure. We are all so short of time and energy. Children need a community with not just one or two but many adults. They learn to share a sense of togetherness with older people who have time to care.'

Erika translated as best she could. Janet nodded, then found herself weeping. She borrowed a handkerchief from Erika.

The three godparents were asked to come to the altar and make their promises. First the Swedes: Ingrid's 'Yes' rang out strongly, Lars's voice was happy and light.

Jack was addressed in English, and made his promise.

'Why are you so sad?' Erika whispered to Janet.

'I'll tell you later,' Janet whispered back. She was thinking of

Jack, whose divorce meant that he would not see his children at all now.

The moment of the christening had come. Elisabeth carried Laila to the font and handed her to Olof. Holding her, he gently stroked the water over her head, in the name of the Father and of the Son and of the Holy Spirit. Then the names were spoken: Laila Elisabeth Viktoria.

The baby's eyes were round with surprise, but she did not cry.

They sang another hymn together, about God's glorious earth.

Then Janet saw her new friend, the organist, quietly walk over to the piano. She felt frightened but, at the same time, icily calm.

When the last verse of the hymn died away, she was ready. Standing by the altar, tall and straight, she began:

> 'Then sings my soul, my Saviour God, to Thee:
> How great Thou art, How great Thou art!
> Then sings my soul, my Saviour God, to Thee:
> How great Thou art, How great Thou art!'

She moved down the aisle, half walking and half dancing, swaying rhythmically from side to side, her voice rising to the roof vaults. She did not forget to wait for the echo.

As usual at this time of day, the cathedral was full of people: tourists who wanted to see it, people looking for peace and to pray in one of the chapels, a group of young singers on their way to a choir practice.

Janet's singing stilled and silenced them. When she had walked back up the aisle and bowed to her audience, the cathedral was filled with applause. Then there were cries of 'Encore!'.

She looked at Olof. 'If you can,' he said.

Her voice rose again:

> 'Then sings my soul, my Saviour God, to Thee:
> How great Thou art, How great Thou art!'

Afterwards many people were waiting for her, wanting to shake her hand and thank her. Finally she was allowed to step out into the sunshine.

She almost fell into the back of Olof's car.

41

The christening party was held at both houses in Oxel Street, with a buffet set out in each kitchen and plenty of wine and beer.

Jack had been looking for Katarina but she had disappeared. The baby had begun to cry, tired by the morning's excitement.

Elisabeth found them and offered to babysit. 'She didn't take much,' Katarina said. 'There's a bottle in the fridge if she gets fretful.'

'We'll be fine. You go and talk to your guests.'

Katarina bumped into Jack on the stairs. 'Let's talk soon. I'll just welcome everyone and then I'll meet you in Mama's sitting room upstairs,' she said.

She hugged and kissed many of her guests but her eyes were searching for Janet. Olof noticed and told her that Janet and Ed were in Viktor Emmanuel's studio. Ingrid was showing them some of his paintings.

'OK. I'll go and talk to Jack now.'

At last they were alone together again. The door to the bedroom where Elisabeth and the baby were resting had been left ajar.

They sat down and he leant towards her, his elbows on his knees, his face close to hers. She observed its bitter lines and the dark rings under his eyes. He's still attractive, she thought.

'You look lovelier than ever,' he said.

'They tell me that giving birth improves your looks,' she replied.

He did not smile.

Silence.

'Perhaps we don't have much to talk about after all,' Katarina said. Suddenly she felt able to say what she had planned. 'We had a wonderful summer together. It was magic, but nothing more. It was a game, not reality.'

'For me it was my only encounter with reality, with life as it should be lived and with . . . love.' His voice broke.

Katarina looked into his eyes and realized that he was speaking the truth. But reality was so threatening you almost had to kill me, she thought. Aloud she said, 'I have found a friend here who had a long, stable marriage and who tells me that that kind of love is like the unspoken communication between two connected vessels. You know everything about your partner – where he is, what she feels – without the need for words. You think in parallel. There's a Swedish poem that begins: "Your cold hands are my hands". That's what love is.'

Jack shook his head. 'It sounds so claustrophobic.'

'I suppose I thought so too, at least in the beginning. I tried to fight it. Now I think it would be lovely to live without secrets, but also that perhaps I'm not mature enough yet.'

'I don't believe in all that,' Jack said.

'So, you see, you and I could never live together. Neither of us has the slightest idea what the other is thinking or feeling. We've never been able to communicate in any way except through our bodies.'

'You don't even want to give us a chance?'

'No, Jack. We're too different. We'd make life hell for each other. I worry about the kind of person I might turn into – defensive, angry, bitter and disappointed. It's important that we both stay true to ourselves.'

'Katarina, I understand all that. I guess I hoped against hope that love would conquer all.'

Katarina thought seriously about this, then said, 'Maybe it's true that love conquers . . . most things – but not all, and one of the unyielding things in my case is fear. I'm afraid because you once took out on me the anger you felt about something that had happened to you with another woman.'

'I believe you're right.' He was very pale.

She continued mercilessly, 'And, you see, I don't want to share that. You'll have to deal with it yourself. Sort it out, or you'll hit some other woman.'

He did not answer.

She added, 'I'm afraid of you now and always will be. I'll never feel safe when I'm alone with you. Even now, with Mama next door and the house full of friends, I feel sick and my heart is pounding.'

He rose to leave the room. In the doorway, he turned and said, 'Please believe me when I say I know how you feel. I'm afraid of myself.'

Then he was gone.

She went in to see Elisabeth, who asked, 'Sad?'

'Yes. But it's over now.'

Katarina stopped on the upstairs landing and listened to the happy party below.

She began to walk downstairs, then stopped again. A thought had struck her. He had never asked about the baby, had not even said that he would like to see her.

She felt better.